THE
Disappearing Jewel of Madagascar

Children's Books by
Sigmund Brouwer
FROM BETHANY HOUSE PUBLISHERS

THE ACCIDENTAL DETECTIVES

The Volcano of Doom
The Disappearing Jewel of Madagascar
Legend of the Gilded Saber
Tyrant of the Badlands
Shroud of the Lion
Creature of the Mists
The Mystery Tribe of Camp Blackeagle
Madness at Moonshiner's Bay
Race for the Park Street Treasure
Terror on Kamikaze Run
Lost Beneath Manhattan
The Missing Map of Pirate's Haven
Downtown Desperadoes
Sunrise at the Mayan Temple

WATCH OUT FOR JOEL!

Bad Bug Blues
Long Shot
Camp Craziness
Fly Trap
Mystery Pennies
Strunk Soup

www.coolreading.com

Accidental DETECTIVES

THE
Disappearing Jewel of Madagascar

SIGMUND BROUWER

BETHANYHOUSE

MINNEAPOLIS, MINNESOTA

The Disappearing Jewel of Madagascar
Copyright © 2002
Sigmund Brouwer

Cover illustration by Chris Ellison
Cover design by Lookout Design Group, Inc.

Published by Bethany House Publishers
11400 Hampshire Avenue South
Bloomington, Minnesota 55438
www.bethanyhouse.com

Bethany House Publishers is a Division of
Baker Book House Company, Grand Rapids, Michigan.

Library of Congress Cataloging-in-Publication Data

Brouwer, Sigmund, 1959-
    The disappearing jewel of Madagascar / by Sigmund Brouwer.
      p.   cm. — (Accidental detectives)
Previously published: Wheaton, Ill. : Victor Books, c1990.
Summary: Twelve-year-old Ricky finds faith is a two-way street when he
is suspected of being involved in the theft of priceless antique jewels and
his friends appear to turn against him.
    ISBN 0-7642-2565-0
    [1. Friendship—Fiction. 2. Christian life—Fiction. 3. Mystery and
detective stories.] I. Title.
    PZ7.B79984 Di   2002
    [Fic]—dc21   2002002813

SIGMUND BROUWER is the award-winning author of scores of books. He speaks to kids around the continent in an effort to instill good reading and writing habits in the next generation. Sigmund and his wife, Cindy Morgan, divide their time between Tennessee and Alberta, Canada.

For Olivia
and the sunshine
you bring into this world.

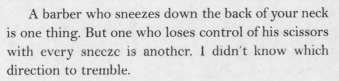

CHAPTER 1

A barber who sneezes down the back of your neck is one thing. But one who loses control of his scissors with every sneeze is another. I didn't know which direction to tremble.

"Aaaaaaaah ... aaaaaaaah ... aaaaaaaah—"

I closed my eyes and hoped for the best. In a barber chair, there's no place to run. They wrap you tight in towels and a plastic covering that somehow drives itchy hair straight underneath and seals it against your skin.

"—choooooooooooo!"

Mr. Breton's scissors shot ahead wildly and chomped shut as his entire body jerked with the sneeze. A big wad of hair dropped into my lap. My hair.

"I could always come back next week, sir," I volunteered.

"Id's otay, Ritty," he sniffed. "I doaned mind working wid a code."

"Really, it would be no problem for me to come back later," I insisted.

Mr. Breton stopped to honk his nose into a tissue. "I already tode you," he said with a trace of irritation. "Yoe ear is fine. Id's only a liddle nick. Id's hardly bleeding any moe."

Wonderful, Ricky Kidd, I told myself. *It's not even ten o'clock on a Saturday morning, and already you have a Band-Aid on your left ear and two bald spots above your right ear. How can the day get worse?*

Easy.

Mr. Breton had a sneezing fit that left me with a head like a scalded porcupine. I noticed a newspaper standing open by itself in a waiting chair on the other side of the barber shop. With giggles echoing from behind it. And a teddy bear beside it.

Joel, my six-year-old brother.

I groaned to myself. Hadn't I lost him by doubling back through Mrs. McEwan's hedge and parking my bicycle at Mike's house as a decoy?

I'm twelve, but Joel terrifies me. Somehow he appears and disappears like a tiny ghost, and at times I least expect or want him. Just when I've fooled everyone, found a spot to relax, he's there, staring at me with those solemn eyes. I nearly burst my skin with surprise, and when I turn my head for a second, he's gone again. Locked doors and walls don't stop that kid.

Fortunately, he does have one weakness. His teddy bear. Battered brown with gray-white paws and a white button for the left eye and a black button for the right eye. When Joel's asleep, you can have a band playing in his room, or wave a good-smelling hot dog under his nose, and he won't wake up. Wriggle one paw of his teddy bear and he sits up instantly, staring at you with big, accusing eyes.

When I'm mad at Joel, I remind him that teddy bear stuffing is hard to replace. It gets his attention. But I could never hurt the bear because I remember Joel's face the day Old Man Jacobsen's dog snuck away with it. Joel began digging in all the dog's favorite hiding spots with his plastic toy garden shovel. He wouldn't let me help. Even the dog was smart enough to stay out of sight. Joel's face was muddy with tears and dirt by the time he found the teddy bear. Then he gave it to me to wash, and we were both happy.

I wasn't happy, though, to see him sitting there enjoying my lousy haircut. Joel was sitting on his knees in the chair, and his tiny fingers were barely noticeable as he held the pages up, so it did look like the paper stood by itself. Even Mr. Breton jumped to see the paper standing tall and shaking to the rhythm of ghostly giggles.

I lost another patch of hair.

For the rest of the haircut, Joel peeked around the edge of the paper after each sneeze, stared solemnly, then hid behind the paper to giggle again.

I sighed. It was nearly ten o'clock already, the time Mrs. McEwan wanted me to stop by her house. Which left no time to lose Joel before I got there.

Mr. Breton sneezed twice more. Big, big sneezes. I wondered if wearing a paper bag to school on Monday would be enough to hide the damage.

Mrs. McEwan stared at my hair from her half-open front door. "Oh, it *is* you, Ricky," she said, then she shook her head slowly as she took in my haircut. "I can never keep up with the things you kids do for fashion these days."

I didn't care to correct her. Mrs. McEwan had a stern face under a thick crown of wavy gray hair. She was a big woman, dressed in a dark suit that was highlighted with a diamond necklace, even though it was early on a hot spring Saturday. She had the look of someone who was accustomed to being obeyed instantly, even by the snobbiest waiter in the most expensive restaurant.

"Thank you so much for stopping by," Mrs. McEwan continued as she motioned for us to step inside her house. "And how nice you are, bringing Joel with you. Most boys your age ignore their younger brothers."

If only I had the choice. I hadn't been able to find a way to lose him on the way here.

She walked ahead of us. As Joel and I followed slowly, I stared at everything around us.

No matter how many times I'd been in her house—usually every second or third Saturday to do some odds-and-ends work, ever since she had fired her gardener a year and a half before—it always amazed me.

Mrs. McEwan is the wealthiest person in our town of Jamesville. Which might not mean much, because Jamesville is a small town, but from what I see and what I've heard, her wealth would set her apart in big cities, too. I've heard Dad talk about her husband, that he died from a heart attack. Mr. McEwan had been a real-estate developer and left her a lot of money plus a good insurance policy.

The McEwan house was a legend in Jamesville. It had been built at the turn of the century by an eccentric—which is just a polite word for crazy, as Mrs. McEwan often explained about the house's first owner—writer who had made a fortune writing old-fashioned books about ghosts and spies.

It was a tall house, three stories high, that reminded me of a castle. Mrs. McEwan said the writer built it to look like that because he was crazy and never really knew if he was in the real world or in his book world, where houses were big and creepy and filled with secret passageways.

To add to the spookiness, long vines of ivy climbed the sides in all directions. It was set on a huge yard, a sprawling lawn with old towering oak trees.

Inside, luxurious rugs partly covered gleaming hardwood floors. All the furniture and cabinets, too, were made from gleaming wood. And magnificent oil paintings and velvet drapes covered the walls from room to room.

Mrs. McEwan continued her stately walk into the dining room.

I entered with Joel. And gasped.

Not at the rows and rows of china on display in a tall cabinet that stretched the length of one wall. Not at the polished silver of tea sets, coffee pourers, and serving utensils stored on a shelf beneath the china. Not at the bronze statues atop the cabinet. Not at a heavy oak dining table that seemed as long as a bus.

I gasped again and grabbed Joel by the back of his collar to hold him back.

Sunlight poured between the heavy velvet drapes of the dining room and spilled and bounced across a small pile of sparkling jewelry set on a cloth in the middle of that oak table.

Yet it wasn't even the pile of glittering light that made me gasp. What drew the breath from me was one jewel—as big as a walnut and a deep, fiery red from the morning sun— set beside a small pair of tongs.

"Antique jewelry," Mrs. McEwan announced simply. "It's been a secret of mine for a long time, but now I want to sort it, reinsure it to its proper value, and display it somewhere. Especially now that I've managed to obtain the treasure of my collection, the Jewel of Madagascar."

Joel pulled. I knew he wanted to play with the pretty stones. I kept a firm grip on his collar.

"The Jewel of Madagascar," I repeated with awe. She didn't have to tell me which one it was.

Joel pulled harder. "Is it okay if I send Joel into your kitchen to play with one of your cats?" I asked. If he wasn't distracted soon, he'd find a way to get me in trouble.

Mrs. McEwan nodded.

I pointed Joel in the right direction and whispered softly,

"Give them a good scare, will ya?" Knowing, of course, that he wouldn't. He likes cats. I don't. Mrs. McEwan has five cats, all of them fancy purebreds. They're long-haired, fat, lazy, and scared of me.

Joel was happy to leave the jewels behind for a dumb cat somewhere else. "Such a nice brother you have," Mrs. McEwan smiled. When she smiled, her face warmed considerably.

"My favorite," I said. I don't have any other brothers. Just a baby sister, Rachel.

I stared at the jewels again.

"I don't know much about those types of collections, Mrs. McEwan, but it sure looks like quite something." I moved for a closer look. "This Jewel of Madagascar . . ."

"It's been owned by kings and queens," she said. "It has centuries of legends surrounding it. Go ahead. Pick it up."

I did so. Gently.

It seemed to glow from my fingers.

"I would have used the tongs," she said, smiling.

"Why?"

"First tell me you don't believe in curses," Mrs. McEwan whispered with a glint in her eye.

"Um, no," I said nervously.

"Good," she replied. "Because this jewel has a tragic past. And the last queen to own it, nearly two centuries ago, put a curse on anyone who dared hold the stone."

CHAPTER 2

Wonderful. A nicked left ear, a scalped head, a kid brother who followed me everywhere, and a curse put on me by a long-dead queen. Who could ask for more on a warm spring day?

Mrs. McEwan continued. "As you may have guessed, the jewel came from Madagascar. Centuries ago, the ruling kings there had many wives. One king gave this jewel to his favorite wife."

The stone felt warm against my fingers. Or was that my imagination?

"But this stone is so beautiful," I protested. "Why would the queen put a curse on it after he gave it to her?" I was quick to add, "Not that I believe in curses, of course."

Mrs. McEwan laughed. She extended her hand away from her, arching her fingers, and examined her fingernails. She buffed them against her shoulder. "You have a few things to learn about women. The queen who *received* it wasn't mad. It was the king's first wife, the one he took it from, who became furious."

"He took it from one and gave it to the other?"

Mrs. McEwan nodded. "Obviously the king didn't know much about women, either."

I set the Jewel of Madagascar down very carefully beside the tongs. From the kitchen, a door banged shut.

"That's Joel," I said quickly, "I'll go get him."

"Don't worry, Ricky. Nothing in the backyard can hurt him."

I never worry about anything hurting Joel. It's what *he* can hurt that makes me nervous.

Of course, I did have something else to worry about, too. "Um, what exactly was the curse?"

Mrs. McEwan wiggled her eyebrows significantly and spoke in a low voice to make it sound evil and mysterious. "To the person who holds this stone, friends become strangers, and strangers become friends."

We laughed at her dramatic voice.

She stopped suddenly. "The crazy thing is the king died two days after the curse."

"Hah, hah. Good one."

"Yes. He laughed at the first queen, held the stone anyway, and two days later, his most trusted adviser led a revolt against him. The friend had become a terrible stranger."

"What about the second queen? She held the jewel, too."

"Even crazier, Ricky. She and the first queen got along famously after that. For her, a stranger became a friend."

"Oh."

"There's more. The stone was lost until the late 1930s. Then British explorers stumbled across it in a village along the Nile, on the African continent. Their leader disregarded the curse, and within a week he had been taken prisoner by his best friend."

"Prisoner? I don't get it."

"They were staying at a nearby army camp because his best friend was a captain. Except it was a German army camp. One week later, war was declared between their two countries, and even though they were far away in Africa, the captain had no choice but to arrest him and confiscate all the archaeological prizes."

The kitchen door banged open and shut again. At least I knew where Joel was. A faint meowing reached us. He'd found the cats.

"All coincidence, I'm sure," I said, staring at the huge red jewel.

"I'm sure, too," she said agreeably. "The jewel recently appeared in a small shop in Paris. Some things lost during the war do that, just appear from dusty boxes hidden in attics or basements. The jewel was then shipped here to the U.S. for an auction. I hope you don't think I'm boasting when I tell you I paid over one hundred thousand dollars for it."

I whistled appreciatively.

"I must say, however, everyone along the way handled it with tongs. You're the first to actually touch it."

My face must have turned white.

"Don't be silly," she said and grabbed it herself. She held it for several seconds, smiled, and put it on the table again. "I only used the tongs to study it better in the light. Curses don't really exist."

I felt a little better. Then I remembered that Mrs. McEwan had invited me over to do some work.

"I really enjoyed seeing your collection," I said. "Is that what you wanted me to do, help you sort it?"

Mrs. McEwan laughed. "I'm afraid not. That takes a magnifying glass and a lot of specialized knowledge. What I want you to do is meet my nephew at the train station while I stay here this morning."

"No problem," I said.

From behind me, Joel's quiet voice said, "Found this bird under a tree."

There is something about my brother that attracts all animals, wild or tame, to him. I can't walk past the Bradleys' German shepherds without sending them into a barking frenzy. Joel can actually walk into their yard and scratch their heads.

I turned to see what he had.

A crow.

And trailing behind him, staring upward in fascination at Joel's hands, were Mrs. McEwan's five ugly, fancy, purebred cats.

"A fledgling!" Mrs. McEwan said. "Sometimes this time of year they want to fly so badly they leave the nest a little too early."

The crow sat calmly between Joel's tiny hands, watching me with unblinking black eyes.

"Here, Ricky," Joel said and reached ahead to offer the crow to me.

That's when the first two cats made their moves. Fat and lazy or not, they leaped upward with outstretched claws just as I was taking the crow.

Four sets of talons raked across my knuckles. One tiny but very sharp crow's beak jabbed at the cats but instead stabbed squarely underneath my thumbnail. I landed on the tail of another cat, who yowled and took a chunk out of my ankle.

All of that was the good part.

The crow popped out of my hands and landed on the dining room table. It cocked its head once, hopped forward, and picked a glittering diamond from the pile. Two cats made it onto the tabletop and leaped at the crow, scattering jewels everywhere.

The crow made it five feet straight upward and beat its wings frantically to stay airborne, somehow making it to the top of the cabinet to caw in triumph at the cats. Then it stopped in amazement and watched as the diamond from its mouth hit the floor. The cats lost no time in jumping from the table to the cabinet, rocking the china inside.

I started moving toward the cabinet.

"Ricky, just leave it!" Mrs. McEwan exclaimed quickly. "There's too much chance that—"

I was so determined to be a hero that I ignored her command. My feet and hands were already in full motion, and I did manage to beat the cats to the crow. I grabbed at it and caught one leg.

It cawed in rage and flapped hard to pull away, knocking a small statue over. I grabbed for the statue with my other hand, still holding on to the crow's leg. Instead, I knocked another statue over, which hit my shoulder and bounced downward and away. Another cat landed on my hand, raking in a new set of claw marks.

There was a loud crash of the statue landing on the table. The crow slipped free as I grunted and fell backward. From the ground, I watched it hop twice to the edge of the cabinet, then spread its wings and coast down to Joel's shoulder.

I also watched one of the cats lose its balance at the top edge of the cabinet and scramble for a moment against the side. But it gave up and let go when it saw a soft landing place. My lap.

Ooooof. I sat straight up and banged my forehead and eye into the edge of the table.

I moaned.

When I finally wobbled to my feet, Joel had the crow cupped in his hands and was stroking its head to calm it. He shot me a dirty look for getting it into trouble.

All five cats were at Joel's feet again, staring hungrily upward. And Mrs. McEwan stood with her mouth covered by both hands, wide-eyed and struck silent with shock.

I turned my head to see what had caused her shock. Then nearly fainted.

The Jewel of Madagascar was still on the table beside the tongs. But half of the remaining jewels on the table had been crushed to tiny bits by the fall of the bronze statue.

CHAPTER 3

What can you possibly say after smashing some-one else's opals and diamonds into worthless pebbles and powder?

I said nothing. Instead, I sat down slowly, trying to absorb the horror.

Twice Mrs. McEwan opened her mouth to speak, but no words came from her, either. Almost blindly, she groped her way to the chair beside me and sat down.

We both stared at the ruined fortune on the table.

Finally she spoke, in such a daze, her voice was almost dreamy. "I've never liked that statue."

I wanted to say the same thing about her cats. My life was ruined. I could not imagine how much that antique jewelry had been worth. I only knew that to pay it back would take much more than cutting her lawn every day for the next forty years. I felt sick about the damage I had caused by trying to catch a stupid crow.

Mrs. McEwan sighed. "Don't worry, Ricky. The Jewel of Madagascar is still safe. And the collection was insured. Only—"

She stopped suddenly.

My heart, already buried somewhere below my

feet, dropped farther.

I said without hope, "Only?"

"Only, I was about to reinsure them." Her voice, usually very alive, became dull. "Their value had risen considerably, and the old insurance policy fell far short of covering their true worth."

I closed my eyes as the significance of the ruin of my life sunk in.

Much as I wanted to, I couldn't blame Joel. He, after all, had found a fledgling crow and saved it from cats in the back-yard. Much as I wanted to strangle the cats, they, too, had only done what cats always do. No, it was my fault, being so clumsy among the statues.

"I'll pay you back somehow," I said. "It just might take a while."

Mrs. McEwan rose slowly and put the statue back atop the cabinet. "Ricky, I appreciate what you're saying. But we should face the truth. There might be tens of thousands of dollars lost on that table. You simply can't pay it back."

In the silence that followed, something unexpected happened.

Joel forgave me for scaring the young crow.

He, of course, had no idea how valuable the pretty stones might be. But he could sense my sadness.

Usually, when I do something that upsets him, he'll stare at me with solemn eyes for days. Like once he smuggled some tamed mice into church. I had to take them from him during the middle of the service. When they got away and caused a panic that sent old ladies scattering among the pews, Joel stayed mad at me for a week.

This time he moved forward, still holding the crow, and peered at my hands. "Do they hurt?" he said with true sympathy.

He was right. My knot of gloom had driven away all the pain. But the deep scratches on the backs of my hands suddenly began to burn, and I noticed my shoulder throbbing where the statue had first landed.

I nodded to him and his eyes widened in sadness.

Joel slipped away from the dining room. With the crow. All five cats turned and followed him, their tails twitching high in anticipation.

So I sat there heavily, doing nothing as Mrs. McEwan first gathered the jewels that had fallen to the floor, then sorted through the broken jewels on the table.

"I understand the opals breaking," she said. "They're softer stones. But the diamonds? That statue must have hit them exactly like a diamond cutter's chisel. I'm almost afraid to look."

She counted through the pile twice.

"Six," she said. "It appears as if three opals and three diamonds were destroyed."

I groaned.

I had to ask. I didn't want to, but I had no choice. "How much?"

Mrs. McEwan ran her hands through her hair. Her face sagged with weariness, and suddenly she looked old.

"I can't tell you immediately, Ricky. I'll have to go through my papers. Each one, you see, is individually insured, and the difference between value and insurance money differs from jewel to jewel."

She straightened. "I almost forgot. My nephew! His train is about to arrive. Will you still go meet him?"

"Of course," I said. "What does he look like?"

The question caught Mrs. McEwan off guard. "I don't know," she began. "He's a . . . a . . ." She finished her sentence quickly. "He's what I call a long-lost nephew. My sister moved away when the boy was very young, and I haven't seen him since he was a baby."

"Oh," I said politely. All I knew about her background, from the times I had been doing chores in the McEwan house, was that her sister called long distance often. "Mrs. Derby? The sister who lives in California?"

She thought for a second, distracted by the mess around her. "That's right. He's been traveling and is just stopping here for a rest. I'm sure, since so few passengers get off the train in Jamesville, that you will have no problem finding him."

I wanted to ask another question, but Joel returned and interrupted both of us. The crow was perched on his shoulder, enjoying its ride and ignoring the hungry cats swarming below it. Joel's teddy bear was still tucked into his shirt, and he was carrying a damp cloth.

Before I could stand or even say a word, Joel reached my chair. He gently started wiping the blood from my scratches.

The crow on his shoulder was directly at my eye level, barely six inches away, as Joel clucked in sympathy over my scratches.

The crow tilted its head and stared back at me. Then it bowed up and down and cawed.

I didn't know whether to laugh or cry.

CHAPTER 4

Halfway to the train station, I heard behind me the thunderous roll of skateboard wheels over concrete.

I knew if I turned my head, I would see a blur of color. Mike Andrews, in mismatched hightop sneakers and a gaudy Hawaiian shirt, blasting his way down the sidewalk. Far behind him, and much more slowly, would be Ralphy Zee, skinny, shirt far too large and hanging over his pants, hair sticking straight up.

I wasn't in the mood for friends.

Joel, I'm sure, was following somewhere nearby. Even though in my deep grief I had broken tradition and actually *invited* him to go the train station, he was staying out of sight as he followed me. Some habits are hard to break.

In theory, then, I was alone in my misery as I went to meet Mrs. McEwan's nephew.

Until Mike slowed his skateboard behind me and stopped by pushing into my back.

"Hi, Mike," I said without turning around.

"Knew it was me, huh?" he said from behind my shoulder. "Why aren't you yelling and screaming like you usually do when I use you for brakes?"

I kept walking.

The second skateboard arrived. There was a scuffling sound of shoes on concrete that I recognized as Ralphy stumbling to a stop.

Still I kept walking and ignored them. A person has a right to sorrow in private.

The rolling of skateboards began as they tried keeping up.

"What's with him?" Ralphy asked.

"Look at his head," Mike explained.

The skateboards rolled in rhythm behind me. Silence as they studied my scalp.

"Haircut," Mike said. "At least I think so."

"Is that a Band-Aid on his ear?"

More silence, except for the slow rolling of wheels.

Then Mike's voice again. "Yup. He *did* get a haircut. Definitely a Mr. Breton special."

Ralphy said, "I'd be depressed, too."

A block ahead, halfway between me and the train station, I recognized a girl pushing someone in a wheelchair. Lisa Higgins. Coming in my direction.

Wonderful, I thought. *A class reunion and me looking like I am dressed for Halloween.*

I continued walking and kept my head high.

Finally Mike scooted in front of me and grinned in my face.

Red hair. Freckles. The perpetual New York Yankees baseball cap. A grin as wide as a Halloween pumpkin and hard to resist by anyone from old ladies to grumpy teachers to best friends.

I resisted it today. It isn't every day you manage to get scalped, cursed by an ancient queen, and land into debt that would probably be tens of thousands of dollars.

Mike planted himself in front of me.

I tried walking around him.

He sidestepped to block me. Ralphy joined him.

We all studied each other gravely. I was in no mood to be cheered.

We studied each other more. I had no intention of breaking the silence.

Then, without speech, Mike swept his cap from his head and bowed elegantly, showing me the top of his head.

That did it.

Despite the misery that was rightfully mine, I burst out laughing. His haircut was worse than mine.

Mike rubbed his scalp ruefully and said, "At least Mr. Breton didn't slash my ear. That must have been a killer."

"Worse," I said. "Joel snuck in to enjoy the massacre."

Mike shrugged. "Ralphy was there for mine."

"I hope I don't look as bad as you," I said. "Breton must have gone into an absolute sneezing fit."

Mike nodded. In places, the white of Mike's skin showed where gashes of hair had been removed.

"My haircut's not the worst of it, pal," I said.

Ralphy looked at me carefully. "He's not kidding, Mike. Something bad has happened."

"Worse than bad," I began to explain. As I reached the part about the bronze statue falling, Lisa Higgins arrived with the wheelchair. She was pushing old Mrs. Ghettley, who had a small bag of groceries in her lap.

"Hi, gang," Lisa said. "Great day for a haircut."

"Ah. Ah," Mike said and quickly put his cap on again.

Lisa is the kind of girl who drives you nuts. First of all, she's good at sports. Of course, we can't let her know it. Mike says it's luck whenever she hits a home run, but I know better. Lisa's the type of person who watches baseball on television to learn from the best, and then practices the techniques she sees until she's ready to use them against us.

Worse, she's pretty, with long dark hair. When she smiles, it's sunshine breaking through clouds. Her smile is so nice to see, there are times when she hasn't made me look stupid for a while that I look for ways to put that smile on her face. Not that I would ever admit it to Mike or Ralphy.

And last of all, every time I do something stupid—like wrecking an antique jewelry collection—she finds out right away.

"Hello, boys," Mrs. Ghettley croaked from her wheelchair in front of Lisa. Ever since she had moved into Jamesville the year before, people in our neighborhood had helped as often as possible. My mom often made her lunches and took them over. And even though Mrs. Ghettley could wheel around by herself, Lisa usually took her to the grocery store on Saturday mornings.

"Hello, Mrs. Ghettley. I was just telling my friends about my accident at Mrs. McEwan's house this morning."

I started my story over again.

As I spoke, I caught Lisa politely looking at my head and looking away again. Stupid haircut.

Mrs. Ghettley didn't notice. But then, she never seemed to notice anything. She was usually in her own world. Always wrapped in a dozen shawls that covered her up to her chin, even on warm days, and another shawl covering most of her head. She chattered endlessly if you had the patience to listen, but rarely heard anything you said in return.

As I described the cats leaping over each other and me, Mike, Ralphy, and Lisa started smirking.

Mrs. Ghettley, of course, was expressionless. She had cupped the fingers of her right hand toward her palm and was examining her bright red fingernail polish.

"It's not funny," I complained. But when I told them about the statue bouncing off my shoulder, they actually laughed out loud.

"Fine," I said. "Do you think it's hilarious that the statue hit the table and busted part of Mrs. McEwan's antique jewelry collection? I'm probably tens of thousands of dollars in debt."

Mrs. Ghettley jerked convulsively. The groceries spilled from her lap onto the sidewalk. A carton of eggs split open and splattered across the tops of our shoes.

"Oh my," she said in the sober silence that followed. "How clumsy of me. You were saying something about Mrs. McEwan's antique bronze table collection?"

"Um, no," I said as Lisa gathered the groceries together. "A jewelry collection."

My reply didn't matter. Mrs. Ghettley was gazing at her fingernails again. The polish was so gaudy that if it were on my nails, I would stare at it, too.

"I nearly forgot," I continued when the groceries were back in Mrs. Ghettley's lap. "On top of all of that, some ancient queen cursed me this morning."

I described the legend and the Jewel of Madagascar.

Mrs. Ghettley stared at me sharply. She noticed me noticing her. "Madagascar. What a quaint name! I knew a cat named Madagascar. It reminds me of the time—"

I coughed politely and interrupted as gently as possible.

"I'm sorry, Mrs. Ghettley. I'm late to meet someone at the train station. I hope you can excuse me." *Inspiration.* "However," I finished, "I'm sure Mike and Ralphy are dying to hear about it."

I left them there as she launched into her story. I didn't want to be the only one suffering that morning.

"Hello, sir," I said along the train tracks in the shade of the station's overhanging roof. "You must be the long-lost nephew."

Six feet tall, I guessed. Light blond hair, a long, lean face with a few days' growth of beard, broad chest under a faded sweater, blue jeans, and a single travel bag resting at his feet. Around thirty years old, I thought.

"Long-lost nephew?" His face went blank for a moment. "Oh yes. Jane McEwan ... that is, Aunt Jane. How is she?"

Adding up my years of debt, I wanted to say. What came out was "Fine, sir."

"Good, good," he said absently as he scanned in all directions. Suddenly his eyes widened as he stared behind me.

I didn't look. "A crow, sir?"

He nodded.

I had been wondering when Joel would appear. Probably glided out from behind a garbage can and made it look like magic.

"That's my brother, Joel," I explained. "He follows me everywhere. He found the crow this morning. I'm sure Mrs. McEwan will tell you all about it. My name is Ricky Kidd."

I stuck out my hand.

The man only stared at Joel.

I finally turned to look. Joel had taken the handkerchief from his teddy bear and tied it loosely around the crow's neck.

I sighed.

"Ricky Kidd, sir," I repeated to introduce myself. "I'm here to take you to Mrs. McEwan's house."

"Oh. Yes." He shook my hand loosely, then picked up his travel bag. "Edward Derby. Glad to meet you."

Some grown-ups are warm to you, treat you like a real person. Some don't care that you exist. Some treat you like a dumb kid. This one was doing none of that.

He noticed me, all right. Just like with his piercing eyes he soaked in every detail of the train platform, the people walking around us, the low-slung buildings of Jamesville, and the quiet streets. It almost made me nervous, as if he were a panther carefully surveying new territory.

To break the silence and to show him I was more than

just a stranger to his aunt Jane, I said, "It's nice that your mom calls often. I know Mrs. McEwan likes hearing from her."

He looked at me oddly, then nodded.

I had a crazy hunch. Maybe it was the antique jewelry collection fresh in my mind, that it was worth so much money. Maybe it was the way he stumbled over the words "Aunt Jane." Or maybe it was his odd look.

I said, "New Mexico, isn't it? Your mom lives close by the mountains there if I remember right."

He focused on me, paused briefly, and came to a decision. "That's correct," he said. "She has a great view from her back porch."

Electricity burned through me.

My hunch was right. This man was not Mrs. McEwan's nephew. She had told me her sister lived in California.

Right then I knew I had two important goals. One, I had to pay for my damage to Mrs. McEwan's jewels. And two, I had to keep the jewels safe from whatever game this con artist had arrived to play.

CHAPTER 5

"Mike," I said in my backyard the next afternoon, "last night I prayed for at least ten minutes."

We had all gone to church in the morning. I had received odd looks there because of my black eye from sitting up into Mrs. McEwan's table, the scratches on my hands, and, of course, Mr. Breton's haircut.

Mike looked at me gravely before he replied. "You know that saying 'Walk with the Lord'? You shouldn't take it literally."

"What!"

"Don't walk while you're praying. By the bump on your head, it looks like you run into things when your eyes are closed."

"Be serious, okay?" I said, rubbing my head where the cat had made me bang it against the table. "You know that happened yesterday at Mrs. McEwan's house, and look, when I have questions about God, it's not time for jokes."

"I'm sorry," he said.

"Maybe you can help, too, Ralphy," I said. "It's been bothering me all morning."

Mike, Ralphy, and I were sitting under the big tree near the garden. Joel was nowhere in sight. Of course, for him that's very usual.

My most pressing concern was money. Twenty-five hundred eighty-five dollars and twenty-five cents. That's what Mrs. McEwan had announced was the difference between the insurance money and the real value of the jewels I had smashed.

My second problem was Edward Derby. You can't just announce that someone is a con artist without proof. So I hadn't said anything. Yet. I would be watching very carefully to find that proof.

I posed my question for Ralphy and Mike. "Should a person pray for money?" I said. "I mean, you know how much damage I did, and that's why we're here to brainstorm a way to get money. But should a person pray to God for help in making money?"

"Why not?" Mike said.

"Because after spending all that time asking God to help me find a way to earn it, I started thinking about people who really need money. You know. People without homes, people without food, people who live in rags. I want this money to pay back Mrs. McEwan, but I don't desperately need it like poor people. So I wondered how selfish it was to waste God's time asking for *my* money."

"I see what you mean," Ralphy said.

"It gets worse," I said. "Because then I started wondering about all the things we ever pray for for ourselves. Maybe we don't have everything we want, but we have everything we need."

I continued. "So when we pray, shouldn't we be concentrating on help for the big things like wars and earthquakes and stuff? Why bother God asking for good grades and no pimples and stuff like that?"

Mike groaned. "Ricky, why don't you shut your head off once in a while? This was looking like a nice, quiet Sunday afternoon." He grinned. "Besides, pal, it's hard to worry about an earthquake across the world when you're holding a test with a big red F across the front."

So much for a serious discussion.

"Fine," I said. "Forget I asked. Help me think of a way to come up with all that money."

"Okay." Mike happily ignored my sarcasm and plucked a long blade of grass and chewed on it. "Before I get serious about relaxing and finding ideas, though, where's your brother and that dumb crow?"

"Mom thought a crow was a little much to handle," I said. "She asked Joel and me to find the nest and return it. The nest was in a corner of Mrs. McEwan's backyard. I climbed the tree and put the crow back. But Joel is allowed to return whenever he wants with bread or cheese to feed him."

"I hope he's feeding the crow now," Mike said. "Not spying on us like usual."

"If not, he'll get bored watching us brainstorm, so don't worry about him."

Mike grinned. "I'm getting bored, too." He pushed Ralphy into the grass and started wrestling. Mike's not real good about sitting and doing nothing for more than five minutes.

I sighed and thought hard of ways to make money. Mrs. McEwan, of course, insisted that I not worry about it. My parents had told me the same thing, that I should pay as much as I could, but not let it ruin my life. But I was determined to pay for my mistake. The only problem was, I didn't know how. *Twenty-five hundred eighty-five dollars and twenty-five cents.* How would I ever—

"I've got an idea!" Mike said. He let go of Ralphy.

"Oh?" It never pays to be enthusiastic when Mike says he has an idea.

Mike jumped up, grabbed a shovel, and frantically began digging in the nearby garden. He wouldn't tell me why until he had ten big, juicy worms. He went to the garden hose and carefully washed them clean of dirt.

"Okay, Ricky," he said, sitting down on the grass. "Move over there about fifteen feet and sit down."

I did.

Mike said to me. "Now open your mouth."

I did.

Mike threw a worm across the space and it banged off my nose before I could duck.

CHAPTER 6

"Are you nuts?!" I shouted across at Mike's grinning face. "That worm could've landed in my mouth!"

"Exactly," he said.

"Exactly?!"

The worm was at my feet, already trying to hide under some blades of grass.

"It's a contest," Mike explained. "Now you throw that one at me. If you get it in my mouth, I have to eat it." He opened his mouth wide.

I was so mad I threw mine without thinking. It smeared Mike's cheek.

"My turn again," Mike said.

"No way," I said.

Ralphy spoke. "What does this have to do with raising money?" he asked.

"Not much," Mike said. "Not much at all. I was just getting bored."

"Forget it," I said. "You're crazy and I hate worms."

"Oh?" Mike raised his eyebrows, the way that makes me feel dumb. "You know what they taste like?"

"No, but—"

"Well, if you don't think you can handle a little

contest like this—"

"I can handle anything you can, pal," I said.

Without saying another word, he threw a worm at me. I tried not to close my eyes. Whap! Right across my neck.

Ralphy only stared from the sidelines.

I was the first one to score. I nearly cried, it made me giggle so much. The worm landed dead center in Mike's open mouth. He screwed his face tight to grimace. Finally, after one or two swallows, it was gone.

Ralphy fell to the grass laughing.

I would've laughed, too, except Mike's next shot landed on my tongue. What do you do with a worm wriggling like crazy in your mouth?

The answer is nothing. I was too paralyzed to swallow, and the worm wiggled there for ten seconds. Mike didn't say anything, just sat and waited for me to choke the worm down.

I closed my eyes and worked up the courage to finally swallow. I imagined that I felt it wriggling in my stomach.

"Yuck!" I said to Mike. "They taste horrible, don't they."

"I wouldn't know," he mumbled. He spit the worm out of his mouth where he'd kept it hidden under his tongue. "I can't believe you actually ate it."

"Aaaaaaaargh!!" I shouted my angriest war cry and jumped up off the grass. Mike has seen me with that look in my eyes too many times. He knew what it meant.

Mike barely made it to his feet in time. He landed running, which was lucky for him, because it gave him a head start.

CHAPTER 7

By the time Ralphy and I reached the corner of the block, Mike had disappeared. We stopped and waited. Sure enough, from one block over came the deep roar of two dogs barking.

The Bradleys' German shepherds. These dogs get upset any time Mike or I try to make life interesting for them. Like when we walk across the top of the Bradleys' fence for a shortcut, or squirt water in their mouths with water pistols. If I were a dog, I'd be thankful for a free drink of water.

Unfortunately, these German shepherds don't look at it that way. They watch for us twenty-four hours a day and announce it to the world whenever we're in the neighborhood, no matter how quiet and nice we are during the times we don't want to be seen by anyone.

"If he passed the Bradleys already, he's making good time," Ralphy said.

"He'd better be. Because we'll feed him so many worms, he'll think it's spaghetti." I looked around. "At least we know his direction. Let's cut him off before he reaches the woods."

Actually, I knew catching Mike would be next to impossible. He's had too much practice at staying out of sight.

Lisa Higgins spotted us on the sidewalk before we could cut across the street. Lisa was on her bicycle, so I hoped she was in a hurry to be somewhere else.

No such luck. When she got near, she hopped off her bike while it was still moving, casually squeezed the hand brake with her left hand, and kicked the bike stand free so that the bike stopped and landed on the stand at the same time. It's something I want to practice, but only if I know Lisa won't be within a hundred miles to catch me doing it.

"Hi, guys. What's up?"

"Not much," I said.

"A worm-eating contest," Ralphy said. "And Mike fooled Ricky into eating a worm."

"Thanks, Ralphy."

"Really?" She gave us the look that girls give guys when they catch us doing something dumb. "And now you want to find Mike."

I nodded.

"If I were Mike," she said, "I'd fool all of you by doubling back to your house."

That girl would drive me crazy.

Sure enough, as Ralphy and I arrived, they were all sitting around the kitchen table. Mike. Joel. My baby sister, Rachel, in her high chair. Tall glasses of milk and stacks of chocolate chip cookies.

I told myself that I should not strangle Mike.

A person can't be perfect all the time. I slammed the door and made a beeline for Mike's neck. He didn't move. But then, he knew he was safe, what with Mom standing in the far corner of the kitchen where I had no chance of seeing her on my way in.

"Oh, hi, Mom," I said with my hands on Mike's neck. "How are you today?"

"Hi, Ricky. Before you strangle people, you should learn to shut the door quietly."

My smile felt silly even to me.

"Busy day today?" she continued. "Worm eating? Chasing people around the neighborhood? You must be tired. Have some cookies and milk."

How do parents know these things? I gave up quietly and accepted both the glass of milk and a short stack of cookies.

Mom sighed, shook her head, picked up Rachel, and left the kitchen.

Mike's brow furrowed and he stared at my neck. "Did you cut through the Thompsons' hedge on the way back here?"

I nodded. "Why?"

"Thought so," he answered. "There's a big hairy spider ready to crawl on your neck. It must have rubbed onto you from the bushes."

"Hah, hah. Nice try, Mike." Leave it up to him to try that old trick. I didn't bother giving him any satisfaction by looking down.

Nothing tastes better than cold, cold milk and the sweet chocolate of cookies on a Sunday afternoon.

"Worm eating," I said in disgust to break the silence. "What could that ever lead to?"

Little knowing how important worm eating would become, I continued. "Can we think about something more crucial? Like making money?"

Mike's eyes widened as I stopped in irritation. For a long time after, I thought his eyes had widened because of what happened next. If only I could have known the truth.

What happened next was more irritation. Something tickling me. I absently opened my T-shirt and looked down.

"Aaaaaaaaaagh!!"

I had never seen a spider that was bigger, hairier, or uglier. And it was crawling straight down to my stomach. The only reason I didn't faint was because I was running.

Mom said later that if I fixed it, she wouldn't be mad at me for knocking two hinges off the screen door.

CHAPTER 8

How do you explain standing under a tree with a teddy bear in one hand, a kid brother in the other, and both your feet frozen to the ground?

What a way to start a Monday. There were less than ten minutes left until the nine o'clock school buzzer rang. It was my daily duty to make sure Joel got to school on time, and here I was, too scared to move.

The teddy bear part is easy to explain. I carry it every morning, as a hostage. Too many things distract Joel on his way to school. If I carry the bear—Mom's idea, of course—and Joel disappears on the way, he will always reappear at the school doors shortly after I do.

On good days, however, Joel actually walks beside me to guard his teddy bear, and only stoops occasionally to politely murmur at interesting bugs.

Getting under the tree is harder to explain.

We had been passing Mrs. McEwan's yard. Joel had stopped suddenly and peered at one of the towering oak trees at the edge of the McEwan property. Which I ignored. The sharpness of Joel's eyes is beyond explanation, and if I worried about every little thing that caught his attention, I'd already be old.

He knew better. In fact, he knew what he was seeing was much stranger than anything he should expect from a grown-up. So Joel had silently pulled me through the hedge, crept to the tree, and pointed upward.

And my feet promptly froze to the ground.

Hidden among the branches, less than fifteen feet above my head, was Edward Derby.

I looked closer, hardly daring to breathe. He was perched on a deer stand—a small platform attached to the tree—and wearing green and brown commando camouflage clothing. Even the backs of his hands were covered with greasepaint.

That was crazy enough.

What really chilled me were the binoculars held steady to his eyes as he intently scanned Mrs. McEwan's house.

He was only one turn of his head away from spotting us. *How long would he keep the binoculars in place? And what would he do when he found us?*

I tugged on Joel's hand, and he turned his questioning eyes to me. I clenched my teeth and grimaced silently, hoping he would understand our need to escape without being seen.

He did.

We began backing away slowly. I wasn't worried about Joel remaining undetected. That's the story of his life.

It was me I didn't trust. Gingerly, very gingerly, I set my feet down for each step. Two steps, five steps, twenty steps. Finally we were away and back to the hedge.

I let the air out of my lungs.

"Why is he doing that?" Joel asked.

"I don't know," I said. "But don't tell anyone. Not yet, okay?"

Joel nodded. Sometimes his trust in me makes me feel warm. Sometimes the responsibility of it scares me. I knew, though, that he wouldn't say a word about this. Which I needed. I wanted time to gather more evidence.

As we ran—the school buzzer would ring any minute—

my brain still churned. Edward Derby. I knew he was an impostor. I now knew he was up to nothing good. And I knew too well how valuable Mrs. McEwan's antique jewelry was. The pieces fit together in an obvious way. But what was he planning to do? And how could I best stop him?

"Hey, Mike!" We had five minutes until the next class began. I was ready to discuss my theory on Edward Derby. Especially since Mrs. McEwan had called just before Joel and I left for school and had asked that I visit her after classes were finished for the day.

Mike turned his head as I skidded to a halt on the waxed floors where he stood by the drinking fountain. Then I noticed the notebook open in his left hand. Which wouldn't normally be strange, but Mike Andrews makes a point of keeping all his books shut between classes.

He snapped the pages closed almost guiltily and hid the book behind his back.

"Um, hi, Ricky."

"What's in your notebook? Plans for a nuclear bomb?" I joked.

"Oh, nothing," he said.

I was too engrossed in thoughts of Edward Derby to dwell on it. So I continued.

"I've got to tell you something, Mike. It's about Mrs. McEwan's long-lost nephew."

"Yeah, sure," Mike said vaguely. He looked over me, around me, and behind me. Anywhere except at me.

"Come on," I said. "It's important stuff and—"

"Hey, Mike!" Ralphy's voice. He came bolting around the

corner and stopped dead when he saw me standing with Mike.

"Oh. It's you." Was that my imagination, or did he sound disappointed?

Mike said to me. "Sorry, pal. Ralphy and I have got to go."

"Where? I'll go with you."

Mike coughed. "We, uh, have to go alone."

With that, both of them turned and walked down the hallway, leaving me with the water fountain.

After school the same thing happened. I caught up to them, but for nothing.

"We've got to go, Ricky," Lisa said before I could say a word. Mike and Ralphy nodded. They, too, left quickly.

And I had an empty corner of the school yard to myself and Joel.

A strange thought came to me, one which I tried to ignore. But it kept coming back. The curse of the Jewel of Madagascar. The jewel I had actually held with my bare hands.

Mrs. McEwan's words echoed in that thought, *To the person who holds this stone, friends become strangers, and strangers become friends.*

Impossible, I told myself.

"Right, Joel? Impossible. Those guys all had violin lessons or something, I'll bet. I'm sure they're still my friends." I snapped my fingers as another thought hit me. "Besides. Edward Derby is the only stranger I know. And he's definitely not becoming a friend."

Joel didn't reply.

I looked around. He, too, was gone. How he does it, I'll never know.

CHAPTER 9

"The good news," Mrs. McEwan began, "is that you're getting a raise. How does one hundred dollars an hour sound?"

I was standing in Mrs. McEwan's kitchen. Before knocking on her door, Joel and I had carefully checked the trees around the house, but we had not seen Edward Derby hidden in any of them. After that Joel had followed me almost to the front doorstep, then disappeared to look for his crow. Which suited me fine.

"A hundred dollars!" I grinned. "If that's true, wondering about the bad news makes me nervous."

Mrs. McEwan grinned back. "It's the truth, Ricky. Your parents and I had a discussion."

So that was the bad news. When grown-ups have a discussion in your absence, you can expect the worst.

I winced, waiting.

"Obviously, almost twenty-six hundred dollars is out of your reach. And we know you'll worry about it forever, because you are insisting on paying it back. So I will pay you one hundred dollars an hour for the chores you do around the house for me."

I started mental calculations. Twenty-five

hundred eighty-five dollars and twenty-five cents. That meant nearly twenty-six hours of work before I was clear. But after that I could get rich. I'd buy—

"Don't get too excited, Ricky. When we're even, you get demoted to your regular three dollars and fifty cents per hour."

"Oh."

With that, she sent me upstairs to paint a small bedroom.

It was okay work, if you like killing your arms by pushing a roller across the ceiling. I had spread plastic all across the floor, so the only thing that could get damaged was my eyes whenever paint dripped into them.

Thinking of damage reminded me to check on Joel.

I glanced out the window.

He was still patiently sitting under the tree that held the crow's nest.

A flicker of movement at the corner of the house caught my eye.

Edward Derby, hidden among the bushes around the walls of the house!

I watched carefully.

He prowled slowly from bush to bush, peering closely at the house and then checking in all directions before moving to another bush.

That did it.

Snooping is dishonest. But so was posing as a long-lost nephew to steal someone's jewelry. I decided it was time to look for clues.

First, I put down my roller and listened for Mrs. McEwan. Without evidence, it was not time to mention my suspicions. I wanted to be sure she was downstairs.

She was. I could hear the banging of pots and pans in the kitchen.

Second, I took another look out the window to make sure Edward Derby was outside in the bushes. He was. I figured that even if he quit prowling and came inside, he would have to stop in the kitchen to say hello. That gave me, I guessed, four minutes, even if he entered the house immediately.

Things looked safe.

I stepped into the hallway and quickly dashed to the room that I knew Mrs. McEwan had assigned to him.

Then I dashed out.

My hands! I had white paint on my hands. Anything I touched would betray me by the paint I left behind. Quickly, very quickly, I scrubbed them clean in the bathroom down the hall.

Then I rechecked Derby's location. Still safe.

Once back in his room, there was not much to see beyond the hardwood floor, the ornate furniture, and the four-poster bed, which had been made neatly.

I checked the dresser drawers first. I was looking for his wallet or his shaving kit. Anything that might hold his real driver's license or birth certificate or any kind of identification that might give him away.

Nothing.

I yanked open the closet door. It was a huge, dark closet, and his clothes, hanging straight, barely occupied a corner of it.

His travel bag!

It, too, hung neatly.

I began to unzip the pockets.

The first four pockets yielded nothing. I hit pay dirt on the fifth. Envelopes and papers filled it completely.

I took a deep breath and—

The bedroom door creaked behind me!

I jumped and turned.

Only Joel. Staring at me with wide, quiet eyes. He never asks questions, only stares.

I thought quickly. If I could get Joel back downstairs, there would still be time to look through the papers and discover Edward Derby's real identity.

I also knew that the kitchen was a safe place to watch for Derby's entrance into the house.

"Does Mrs. McEwan have cookies for us?" I asked.

Joel's eyes brightened.

I took his hand and guided the both of us downstairs.

Mrs. McEwan did have cookies ready, as she usually did whenever I was working for her.

Joel and I began to munch. I swallowed quickly. I wanted to get back upstairs.

"By the way, Ricky," Mrs. McEwan said, "I don't believe I mentioned I'm going to be at your school tomorrow."

"Really?" I commented, my mind on the closet upstairs.

"I'll be showing my antique jewelry pieces and telling the stories behind each of them. Especially the story about the Jewel of Madagascar."

"That's nice." I gulped my cookie down. "I should get back to work before my paint dries on the roller." Edward Derby had not entered the house yet, and I was anxious to look through those papers.

I dashed up the stairs. I probably should have thought there was something strange about Mrs. McEwan being so determined to make her jewelry collection public after hiding it for all those years, but my mind was on the travel bag waiting for me in that closet.

At the top of the stairs, I took one final look beneath me to make sure that Derby was not somewhere behind me.

I ran into his room. And slipped and fell on a throw rug in the middle of the room as I tried to stop.

Half in and half out of the closet in front of me stood

Edward Derby. He straightened at my crashing arrival and frowned.

I made sure it took five seconds to get back onto my feet again. I needed the time to think.

"Nuts," I finally said. "You'd think I could remember which room needed painting."

I squirmed out of his room before he could reply and painted furiously for the next hour before quitting to go home for supper.

Edward Derby stared at me strangely as I said good-bye to Mrs. McEwan.

CHAPTER 10

"About yesterday," I started immediately after catching up to Mike and Ralphy ahead of me on the sidewalk. "Do you guys think you can explain what was going on? I mean—"

"Look at that!" Mike hissed to Ralphy. "It's a garter snake!"

It was Tuesday morning, and we were on our way to school. We all had knapsacks to hold our books. Mike also had his skateboard in his hands. Ralphy had a computer manual. As usual, I had Joel's teddy bear. And as usual, he was nowhere to be seen.

Ralphy hissed back at Mike. "I hate garter snakes!"

"No, look," Mike said, "It's a big one."

Sure enough, a fat garter snake was about twenty feet away, lazing on the grass in the morning sun. There was no sense in trying to discuss their strange behavior of the day before with such an obvious distraction in front of us.

Ralphy looked in the opposite direction. "I don't see it. I don't see it. I don't see it."

"Come on, Ralphy. They're not that bad," Mike said.

"You try having a bunch squiggle up your pant

legs some day."

Once on the way to summer camp, my brother, Joel, had found some garter snakes and put them into his knapsack. When they got loose on the bus, the first place they found for refuge was Ralphy's pants. He still shakes when he thinks about it.

"Let's catch it," Mike said. "We could put it in Joel's desk and get him back for all the times he has scared us to death."

"Wrong," I said, shaking the teddy bear to remind Mike. "One, Joel's somewhere behind us right now, spying. Two, you know how he is with animals. Even the Bradleys' German shepherds like him. Joel would love to find a snake in his desk. And three, you can be sure he'd get us back twice as bad. By accident."

"You're right," Mike said. "What was I thinking?" He sighed. "It's just that a person hates to waste a perfectly good garter snake."

The snake, I'm sure, thought we couldn't see it in the grass. It stayed there, sassy and fat, the regular kind of spring temptation that makes it hard to sit all day in a classroom.

Of course, I knew it was going to be hard to sit still in class anyway with my thinking about Edward Derby and his suspicious behavior. I was still trying to decide how he had managed to get into his closet without me spotting him pass the kitchen.

"How about Lisa?" Mike asked, tearing me away from my thoughts.

"For a girl, I guess she's okay," I said slowly.

"No, dummy," he said. "Not how is she. How about scaring her with the garter snake."

I rolled my eyeballs. Ralphy shook his head. But we knew we were in trouble. When Mike gets an idea into his head—

"Didn't she hit two home runs off you the Saturday before last, Ricky?"

"Who cares? She threw you out at first three times."

"That's what I mean," Mike said. "If she wants to play boys' games, she should get used to all of them." Mike didn't bother waiting for an answer. He put his skateboard next to Ralphy, snuck up slowly on the snake, then dove!

"Aaaaargh!" It slipped between his legs and slithered toward Ralphy.

"Yipes!" Ralphy jumped, forgetting about Mike's skateboard.

"Aaaagh!" The skateboard slipped under him when he landed, then shot down the sidewalk. Ralphy flailed his way backward to the ground and landed with a thump on the grass. His computer manual made a high arc and landed on Mike's head. The snake made a shift to the right.

I shifted to the left. The only way to deal with developing disaster is to clear the area.

Mike doesn't see it that way. He took a little break to glare at Ralphy in disgust about the computer manual, then made another dive for the snake. And another.

The snake shot back toward Ralphy, and Mike made one last heroic dive. It only made the garter snake squirt right into Ralphy's lap.

For one moment time was frozen. It seemed like Ralphy was etched against the sky, he stood so quickly. The snake was in his right hand, and he was holding it high above his head in disbelief.

Then time went back to normal. Ralphy realized what he was holding and screamed and ran straight ahead in panic. It didn't matter that straight ahead was Mr. Thompson's hedge. I winced and closed my eyes.

The bushes boomeranged Ralphy back into the open. He landed hard enough to make him cough. Slowly, very slowly, Ralphy peeked at both his hands. The snake was gone.

"Good going, Ralphy," Mike said from where he was sitting on the grass and panting. "You let him get away."

I congratulated myself the rest of the way to school. I had managed to remain unhurt and unstained. Ralphy had a few scratches on his arms, and mud and grass clumps on his jeans. Mike had mud and grass and grease from crawling under a car for his skateboard. Plus he had two bumps on his head; one from the computer manual and one from hitting the muffler of the car.

"Let me guess. Mike and Ralphy chased parked cars," Lisa Higgins said as we approached her near the school doors. She was wearing a light blue dress and a large, pale blue ribbon in her hair to match.

Mike grunted. "It's your fault, anyway."

Lisa smiled her mysterious smile, the one she uses when she doesn't understand something but wants to make it look like she actually understands much more than you.

"I'm sure it is, Mike," she said. "Ta ta."

She left us standing near the school doors as we waited for Joel.

"Boy, is she lucky," Mike said. "If I could hide that snake in her desk, she'd have a heart attack. Enough to make her stop smiling like that."

"Yeah, that's too bad," I said without meaning it, relieved to be totally unharmed and—without the snake—safe from any possible blame.

I was still congratulating myself for surviving Mike's latest trouble when Joel appeared from around the corner.

"Can I have my teddy bear now?" Joel asked.

Some people think it's strange that Joel doesn't talk much, and when he does, he says as little as possible. I know it's just Joel. He already knows how to read, and even print out complete sentences, and he knows more words than most kids his age. But he's shy, plus he mispronounces words once in a while, so he gets his out-loud sentences over with as fast as he can. Which means using as few words as possible to be understood.

I nodded. As I handed him his teddy bear, Joel reached into his shirt to give me something in return. He held it gently in both hands.

It was the garter snake.

"You wanted this, right?"

How he does it, I'll never know. Not only had he seen us trying to catch the snake, he found it later and picked it up. And it was calm about being with him. Joel has that magic with animals. It wasn't even wriggling in his hands.

Ralphy yipped and knocked me over running into the school. I landed on the biggest wad of gum on the sidewalk. Mike stepped on my hand walking over me to take the snake from Joel. And Joel disappeared as I shouted in pain.

"Somehow, I'm getting this into her desk," Mike said. He looked at the squiggling snake in admiration.

"Wonderful," I said from my position on the sidewalk.

CHAPTER 11

"Okay, everybody, today we're having a surprise math test."

Everybody in the classroom groaned at the mid-morning announcement. Mr. Evans winced. He is nearly deaf, and when the whole class makes a sudden loud noise, his hearing aid rings.

"But before that, we will have two surprise visitors. Mrs. McEwan, whom most of you know already, has graciously offered to show us her antique jewelry collection. She will be bringing her nephew, Edward Derby. I expect them here any minute."

At least by then I should have asked myself a lot of questions. For starts, why, after keeping her valuable collection a secret for so long, was Mrs. McEwan going out of her way to show it to people? Instead, most of my mind worried about why my friends were treating me so strangely. Twice already this morning Mike had stopped talking to Ralphy as I approached, and each time looked guilty, as if I had caught him doing something bad. And if that weren't enough to worry about—along with the math test—there was the garter snake.

During a break between classes, Mike had managed to sneak the snake into Lisa's desk. If she now opened the lid, it would pop out at her. Mike thought it was hilarious.

Not me. Somehow, I knew I would get blamed for part if not all of it. And getting in trouble was always easier on Mike. He only had one parent to go home to because his mom and dad had split. I had two parents to get upset.

A gentle knock on the classroom door interrupted my brooding thoughts.

When Mr. Evans opened the door, I saw immediately why Edward Derby was along. The jewelry was in a big chest he had to struggle to carry inside.

Mrs. McEwan followed him.

"Mr. Evans," she said. "It's so nice to see you. Edward and I have been having a great deal of fun showing this to all the other classrooms."

Mr. Evans bowed a little, "It's our pleasure, Mrs. McEwan."

Edward set the long wooden chest on a table that Mr. Evans had moved to the front of the room. Then Edward stood back near the chalkboard. He scanned the room, stopping briefly to stare oddly at me.

After Mr. Evans introduced them both, Mrs. McEwan began speaking.

"I'd like all of you to come up here and view these," she said, "but first I'd like to give you some background on the jewelry. Each piece, you see, has a history of its own. My favorite is the Jewel of Madagascar. A long time ago—"

Suddenly she stopped and smiled at me. "Ricky, why don't you tell the story. My throat is a little dry from all my talking already this morning."

Wonderful. And while I was at it, did she want me to tell everybody how to wreck thousands of dollars' worth of diamonds and opals with a crow, five cats, and a stupid statue?

"I'm not too good at telling stories," I tried to protest.

She merely smiled. How do you say no to such a stern-looking woman?

Mr. Evans said, "Would you like to come to the front now, Ricky?"

There is something about standing in front of people that makes a person's legs weak, especially when you have a haircut that looks like it was done with a lawnmower. I knew everyone there in the room, and I was still a nervous kitten walking to the front of the classroom. My throat was dry, and my feet felt like clumps of cement.

I saw that the long wooden box was lined with rich red velvet and each jewel sparkled magnificently. The Jewel of Madagascar gleamed from the center of the collection. I forced my eyes back to the classroom of kids waiting for me to tell the story of the curse.

My dad says that he imagines people sitting in their underwear whenever he has to make a speech. He says that it makes them seem less intimidating as they all stare at him, waiting for him to start talking.

His trick worked in reverse for me. I started thinking that everyone in the classroom was imagining *me* in my underwear. Worse, it felt like Edward Derby's eyes were burning a hole in my back. *Does he suspect I know about him?*

The story of the jewel disappeared as my mind blanked out. I stood there silent for ten seconds, but it felt like a month.

Mr. Evans coughed, "The story, Ricky?"

"Right. The story." I managed to remember bits and pieces of what I wanted to say. "Well, it started with a king on the island of Madagascar a long time ago—"

I stopped in horror. Lisa Higgins was opening her desk lid. Suddenly I wanted it to be thirty seconds earlier, when my biggest problem was remembering how to tell the story of the Jewel of Madagascar.

"Lisa!" I squeaked loudly.

Everybody stared at me. Lisa stopped with her desk lid partly open.

I lowered my voice and finished lamely. "I mean, Lisa already knows the story because she heard it last Saturday."

She frowned at my silliness and shook her head. She opened her desk completely and stuck her head forward to see inside.

I winced, preparing for the scream that would send Mr. Evans' hearing aid into the next classroom. Why does Mike have to do these things?

I was holding my breath in horror. Any second she would—

"Aaaaack!" My shoulder! From nowhere, something hit my shoulder during those awful few seconds as I watched in terror for Lisa's snake. People think Ralphy is nervous, but with a brother like Joel, I'm not exactly calm a hundred percent of the time, either.

The classroom giggled as I landed.

It was Mr. Evans' yardstick. He had moved up behind me while I was staring at Lisa.

He tapped me again. "Ricky, if you have a story to tell, we'd like to hear it. I'd like to give the math test sometime before Christmas."

Everybody giggled again. I didn't say anything. When teachers try to be funny, if *you* say something funny in return, you get in trouble. It's one of the rules in school you learn early.

I stared at Lisa slowly lowering the lid of her desk. Nothing. No snake. No screaming. Just Lisa sitting there calmly and looking cool in her light blue dress.

Mr. Evans interrupted my staring again. "Or, since you find Lisa so interesting, we could move your desk beside hers."

I felt the red start at my Adam's apple and work its way to the tips of my ears.

"The jewel, it is told," I said quickly, "has a curse for any-one who dares hold it."

That distracted everyone from Mr. Evans' comment about Lisa. With the extra breathing space, I continued and described the curse of the Jewel of Madagascar.

As I told it, I looked in desperation for anything green and wiggly in the classroom. The garter snake must have escaped. No telling where it would appear next. *Anybody but Ralphy*, I told myself. *Anybody but Ralphy*. If an open door wasn't nearby, he'd make a hole in the brick wall from run-ning out so fast.

"And so," I finished, looking back into the velvet-lined case, "it's a beautiful jewel, with or without a curse."

I wanted to add that they shouldn't hold it unless they wanted their friends to begin acting strangely, but I didn't believe in curses. Instead, I walked back to my desk.

Mr. Evans said, "Thank you, Ricky. Now we're going to have all of you come up here to look at the collection, but only one row at a time because I want no noise and no confusion. Those of you waiting in the other rows should take out your math books."

I looked over at Mike, about to whisper my message, *The snake has vanished*. I was in the third row, and Mike was in the fourth.

"Mike," I started softly as the first row of kids filed to the front of the room. "The snake is—"

I have never seen anybody run three feet while still sit-ting in his desk. That's exactly what Mike did. He yelped a tiny yelp and began running with his body still stuck in the desk.

Everybody in the room froze.

I think Mike would have yelled loudly if possible, but his face had gone white and he didn't have the energy. His hands were trapped under the desk lid and still his scrambling legs blindly pushed the desk ahead.

He stopped only when the front of his desk rammed Evelyn Beingessner's desk.

She glared at him in the black silence that followed after his desk legs had finished scraping a trail through the floor wax.

Mike yelped again. This time feebly.

The fat garter snake crawled out from between his arms and beelined for the darkness of the coat closet in the back of the room.

Which started more calamity. Most of the girls in the back half of the classroom screamed, stood, and rushed to the front of the room to escape the snake. It was a piercing noise that hurt even my ears. Mr. Evans held his hands over his head in agony.

The snake disappeared into the closet.

The girls stopped stampeding.

Mr. Evans marched down the aisle to Mike's desk, where Mike was still sitting in the frozen position with his arms under the lid.

"There's a good reason for starting a zoo in your desk, right, Mike?"

Mike said, "I didn't put it there! Honest."

Which was true. Mike didn't like lying. He did crazy things once in a while, and he liked kidding around to get Ralphy and me in trouble, but he hated lying.

I had already figured it out, though. Burning in my mind was the one thing that had made the snake look so crazy as it wriggled for safety. A blue ribbon.

I closed my eyes and pictured the snake. Right behind its head, tied neatly in a bow, had been a blue ribbon. The color of the ribbon perfectly matched Lisa's dress.

Lisa, from her desk near the front, was looking back at me to see if I understood. She tossed her hair and it flowed loosely across her shoulders. Then she smiled.

I grinned inside.

And Mrs. McEwan screamed.

CHAPTER 12

She screamed again. A short, ear-piercing shriek.

Mr. Evans, still in front of Mike's desk halfway up the aisle, gently set his hearing aids on the floor, then calmly stepped on them. When he lifted his foot, only tiny pieces of plastic were left.

"Silence," he said to no one. "Silence at last."

"Four diamonds are gone," breathed Mrs. McEwan. She slowly sank into the chair beside her collection.

That made for plenty of silence for the rest of us, too.

"Nobody move," Edward barked to the kids standing at the front of the room.

Mr. Evans walked to the front, smiling peacefully at Mrs. McEwan.

"I've needed new hearing aids for quite some time," he loudly said to her as he pointed at his ears. "All that noise must really have done some damage. Because whatever you were saying came out as a scream."

He happened to glance at the collection.

"Oh no!" he shouted. "Some diamonds are missing!"

He frantically waved at Mrs. McEwan and

pointed at the display. She smiled wanly.

"This is a disaster," he continued as he looked at the floor around everybody's feet. "Where could they be?"

I had a good idea. Edward Derby. There had been enough confusion during the snake stampede for him to pocket them. And it would be easy enough for him as a grown-up to blame someone else in the room.

As if reading my mind, Edward said, "Nobody leaves this room until we find them."

"Broom?" Mr. Evans said. "I don't think a broom is necessary. We'll just find them and pick them up."

A frown crossed Edward's face. "Room, not broom," he said. "Stay in the *room*."

"Of course," Mr. Evans said as if he were dealing with a small child. "This is where I teach."

Derby gritted his teeth and walked close enough to look into Mr. Evans' hairy ears. He cupped his hands and spoke loudly and coldly.

"Nobody leaves this room until we find those diamonds. They're worth a small fortune."

A look of understanding crossed Mr. Evans' face, and then a look of indignation. "Surely," he replied, "you are not suggesting one of my students has stolen those diamonds." He turned and glowered at Edward Derby.

Derby nodded grimly.

"Impossible," Mr. Evans said, his face growing red. "Not these students."

Derby shrugged as he stepped back from Mr. Evans and said, "Maybe, maybe not. But I'm going to the principal's office. He'll help us get to the bottom of this."

"Look, young man," Mr. Evans spoke firmly. "Nobody accuses my students of being thieves. Instead of standing there, I suggest you go to the principal's office. He'll straighten you out."

Edward Derby sighed as he left the classroom.

Except for the fact that Mr. Evans shouted a lot and that everything had to be said two or three times for him to understand any conversation, the search went smoothly.

Mr. Stanley, our principal, a huge man with a ring of red hair around his nearly bald scalp, had returned with Edward Derby and taken control. He had instructed Mike to straighten his desk and then take the garter snake from the coat closet to be released outside.

Then Mr. Stanley had commanded all of us who had been sitting down to leave the room. We, of course, couldn't possibly have taken anything from the collection.

Waiting outside in the hallway, we could hear the repeated shouting at Mr. Evans. It continued for about ten minutes after Mike's return from outside, and then we were invited back into the room.

The look on Mrs. McEwan's face told the story.

The diamonds had not been found. Which didn't surprise me.

"Are you sure the diamonds weren't on Mr. Derby?" I asked Ralphy that afternoon as we left the school grounds. Mike, strangely enough, was nowhere in sight.

Ralphy nodded. Naturally, he had been the first student to reach the front of the class during the snake stampede. He, too, had been asked to empty his pockets, waggle his tongue, and generally prove that the diamonds were not in his possession.

"It was the first thing he did," Ralphy told me for the third time, because I still couldn't believe it. "He said he was not above suspicion, either, and that he should be searched like everybody else in the room. Why do you keep asking?"

Nuts, I told myself for the third time. I was positive that the man who called himself Edward Derby was the one who had taken the diamonds.

I was ready to tell Ralphy what I knew about the man. The way he had lied about his mother living in New Mexico. The way he had spied on Mrs. McEwan's house from the tree. The way he snuck around her house.

"I keep asking," I began, "because there is some stuff I haven't told you. Come over to my house for some cookies and I'll explain."

"Sorry, can't do it," he said. "I've got to go." He started running.

I should have tried to follow, but at that point, I still believed Mike and Ralphy were my friends.

CHAPTER 13

"Here you are, sir," I said to Edward Derby. "A nice glass of Kool-Aid for a hot spring afternoon."

I held the tray out. That was a crucial part of my plan, using a tray instead of my hands to carry his glass.

He looked at me suspiciously as he took the offered glass. "Did Aunt Jane send you out here?"

I nodded. "Of course, sir."

It wasn't exactly a lie. After Ralphy's sudden departure, I had gone to Mrs. McEwan's house to paint. Because of the loss of the diamonds in the school, I was more determined than ever to prove Edward Derby was not Edward Derby. Since his room upstairs had been locked, there was no way to check his closet, even if I dared. I had noticed Edward below trimming a hedge, however, and that had led to an idea. So I had wandered downstairs, asked for something to drink and mentioned to Mrs. McEwan how hot it might be outside. She had taken the hint immediately and suggested I take some Kool-Aid to Edward, too.

Outside the house, I had wiped the glass clean of Mrs. McEwan's fingerprints. The cloth was still inside my pocket.

He caught me staring.

"Don't you have work to do?"

"Hours and hours of it," I said, thinking of how much money I owed Mrs. McEwan. "But it would be silly to bring back an empty tray."

"Yeah, right." He set the glass down and I smiled innocently.

With one final glare, he picked up the trimmers and turned back to the hedge.

Once out of his sight, I took the cloth from my pocket and wrapped the glass, careful not to touch it with my own fingertips.

Mrs. McEwan was not in the kitchen, so that saved me having to find a way to keep the glass while making it look like I was returning it. Because my first stop after supper would be the police station. With the glass. And Edward Derby's fingerprints.

There was, as they say, more than one way to skin a cat.

"Where are you off to tonight, Ricky?" my mom asked conversationally as I finished drying the rest of the supper dishes.

"Cat skinning," I said with a grin, thinking about how to nab Edward Derby.

Unrattled, she replied, "That's nice. Be back by the usual eight o'clock. And be quiet coming in. Rachel will be asleep."

I nodded. That gave me plenty of time. Even if I was going alone.

Forget Mike and Ralphy, I had told myself, remembering their behavior over the last few days. *Who needs them?*

As I reached the back porch, I saw Joel standing over the

paper bag that held the cloth-wrapped glass.

"Sorry, pal," I told him. "You can't be going through that bag. I need it for tonight."

Without saying a word, he dashed out the door.

Not that I was surprised. Everybody, it seemed, was ignoring me lately.

As I skateboarded to the police station, I thought about how people can turn on a person. I mean, Ralphy and Mike and I had been close for years. Suddenly nothing. They were treating me as if I didn't exist. I began to wonder if it was worth trusting anybody. *I'll make it alone through life if I have to*, I told myself.

The Jamesville police station was in the downtown area, opposite the town library. It was a two-story building that our class had toured once. There were jail cells in the back part; we had been expecting to see them full of criminals, but Sergeant Brotsky, a big man with a handlebar mustache, had only laughed back then. "It's a quiet town, kids," he had boomed. "These cells mainly collect dust."

So I knew what to expect upon walking in. A long, wide counter and a quiet hush.

Tonight was no different.

It was Sergeant Brotsky himself who greeted me by rising from his desk behind the counter.

He smiled at first, but when he looked closer and saw my face, the smile twisted slightly.

"Ricky Kidd," he said through the twisted smile.

What a good memory, I thought. The class tour had taken place last fall. But knowing he had a good memory comforted me. That's the kind of person you want for your policeman, especially when you have a fraud like Edward Derby to investigate.

"Yes, sir," I said, "And I have something I'd like some help with. But I would appreciate it if you kept it confidential."

"Certainly," he said, still watching me closely.

It was nice to see such healthy interest.

I held up the bag proudly.

"This, sir, might be the clue toward catching a thief—before he steals."

His big face twitched again. "You don't say."

"Yes, sir. He calls himself Edward Derby."

Suddenly Sergeant Brotsky's face turned red and he started coughing madly.

When he finished, he said, "I'm sorry. My supper sandwiches were quite dry tonight. They catch in your throat, you know."

I nodded sympathetically. I then explained about Mrs. McEwan's jewelry, Edward Derby's strange behavior, the diamonds that had been lost in the school, and lastly, the way he had lied about his mother living in New Mexico.

"So," I finished, "I thought you could check his fingerprints. You know, the way they do on television against the FBI files. I'll bet Edward Derby is a wanted man."

Sergeant Brotsky started coughing again. He caught his breath and looked at the bag. "Are his fingers in there?"

"Good one, sir. It's actually a glass. One that he held this afternoon."

I carefully pulled the glass out of the bag, keeping it in the cloth to avoid getting my own prints on it.

"You are serious about this, aren't you?" the big policeman said. He then stared at me thoughtfully for at least thirty seconds before coming to a decision.

"We'll check it out." He leaned forward. "Have you told any of your friends your suspicions?"

I shook my head no.

"Good. Keep it that way. You may tell your parents, of course, but no one else. Understand?"

This time I nodded yes. "How long does it take for the results to come in?" I asked.

"Depends," he replied. "First we dust the glass. Then we

can send a JPEG of the prints to a computer in Washington. It may take a few days, depending on the work load there. I would guess that we'd hear back by Monday."

Monday.

That seemed like a long time to wait.

CHAPTER 14

"I'll fool everybody in town," Mike was saying to Ralphy. "They'll think I'm eating real worms."

"What's that, Mike?" I asked, coming around the corner and nearly bumping into him as he stood in front of our lockers.

It was Wednesday morning, a few minutes ahead of classtime, and I had just walked into the school.

"Nothing," Mike said to me immediately.

"Worms," I said as I opened my own locker. "You mentioned worms."

"Worms?" Mike had a puzzled look on his face. "Ralphy, did you hear anything about worms?"

Ralphy shook his head.

Mike spoke to me. "I think all that work at Mrs. McEwan's is making your head go soft." He snorted as he shut his locker. "Worms." Then he said, "Let's go, Ralphy."

They left me talking to a slightly battered locker.

"Nice," I said to the locker. "A person might almost think that the Jewel of Madagascar really *has* put a curse on me."

Lisa Higgins stopped beside me, glanced inside my locker, back at me, frowned, shook her head, and started walking again.

I opened my mouth to explain to her retreating shoulders, but down the hallway beyond her, I saw something that made my mouth snap shut again.

Edward Derby! In the doorway that led to the principal's office, talking to Mr. Stanley!

I moved behind my locker door and peered through the tiny vents to watch their conversation. If only I were close enough to hear them.

They spoke for another five minutes.

Mr. Stanley, who often used his hands as he spoke, was a regular windmill the entire time. Finally they shook hands, and Edward Derby strode to the other end of the hallway and left through the main doors.

What could be going on? What could they be discussing that would last so long? What—

Aaaack!

Even before I landed, I knew what had tapped my elbow was Joel.

I took a deep breath before looking into his solemn eyes. "Yes, Joel."

He held out his marble bag. "Keep this for me?"

"Yes, Joel."

I set the marbles on the top shelf of my locker and closed the door. The bell would ring any minute now.

As I was working the combination lock closed, with my heart still pounding from Joel's sudden appearance, I spoke to him. "You're such a banana brain, you know. Next time at least have the decency to cough or something to give me warning."

There was a cough. A deep cough.

I spun around. And nearly poked my eye out on Mr. Stanley's tie clasp.

"Banana brain?" he asked.

Joel, of course, had vanished. How he does it, I'll never know.

Two things don't mix. English and the certain knowledge of impending doom.

I sat through the first hour of class, numbed by spelling and punctuation, contemplating my final moments of life as I knew it. Mr. Stanley had requested I appear in the office at the end of the hour.

He had—as he explained with a sweet smile that I knew meant trouble—arranged for me to miss the first half of my next class. *Just a little discussion,* he had continued, *nothing to worry about.*

Right. And the Joker is president of Batman's fan club. Little discussions for grown-ups usually translate to major problems for the rest of us.

The remaining first hour of class only took a week. Then I trudged to Mr. Stanley's office. His secretary escorted me to his desk.

"Hello, sir."

"Hello, Ricky." He pointed at a chair. "Won't you please sit down."

Photos of Mr. Stanley as a college-aged football player covered the wall of the back half of his office. His desk top, empty of all papers, was a large expanse of dark wood. Mr. Stanley sat back in his chair and contemplated me as he absently scratched the fringe of his hair with a long pencil.

"When I was your age," he began, "I had an old clunker of a bicycle. I painted it each summer. It had big fat tires as I remember. And it weighed a ton. How about you?"

What kind of discussion was this?

Finally I said, "I don't think I'm real heavy, sir. The kid down the street, we call him Backstop Freddy because he's big enough to be a backstop, but—"

"I didn't mean how much do you weigh," he said with a tightening of his lips. "What kind of bicycle do you have?"

"Oh. A mountain bike, sir. Fifteen speeds."

"You see?" he said.

I didn't see.

"Times have really changed. When I was your age, money was hard to find. Especially for children. Now I watch all of you coming to school in designer jeans and playing handheld computer games."

"I don't wear designer jeans, sir. And my mom makes me carry a teddy bear."

Mr. Stanley suddenly leaned forward, a strain on the chair, which made a small popping sound.

"But you do have a new bicycle. And it's worth a lot of money. How about computer games?"

"A few, sir."

He tapped his front teeth with his pencil, then looked at me strangely. "And what else that's worth a lot of money?"

I felt my face scrunch. "I don't understand, sir."

He stared intently at me. *What was he looking for?*

"Forget it."

He stood, reminding me exactly how big he was. He paced around his desk.

"I hear you're trying to pay off a large debt to Mrs. McEwan."

"Yes."

"And you, as I recall, were one of the kids seated when that snake got loose on Tuesday."

I nodded.

He continued, "Your friend Ralphy was at the front."

"He's terrified of snakes."

"And your friend Ralphy has an iMac computer?"

My face scrunched again. It was hard to follow this conversation. "Yes, sir. He spends hours on it."

Mr. Stanley stopped pacing. "Those iMacs are top-of-the-line computers." He stared closely at my face again. "How do you suppose he got the money for it?"

"Sir?"

"Money. How did he pay for it?"

I took a deep breath and thought. "His parents, I believe. They loaned the money to him, and he pays them back a part of it each month from what he makes cutting grass and shoveling sidewalks. He loves that computer."

Mr. Stanley's shoulders slumped. "I'm lousy at this," he muttered.

I remained silent.

"Make this easy on me," Mr. Stanley finally said. "Is there anything you want to confess to me?"

It clicked. *I'm being interrogated!*

I said quietly, "You mean, like I have a nice bicycle because I've been stealing things for years? And Ralphy has a nice computer because he helps me? And somehow we both saw a great opportunity to steal four diamonds?"

"Something like that," Mr. Stanley said, reading the anger in my face. "I'm sorry to have started the questions with you. But four very expensive diamonds were lost in this school, and I have to start somewhere. I'd really hate to have to go as far as searching lockers."

Suddenly I felt sorry for Mr. Stanley. As principal, he would be responsible. I knew too well how much those diamonds were worth.

"Sir," I said, "my locker is just down the hallway. You're welcome to search it."

Strangely, he look relieved. "I'll do that, Ricky, even though I know we won't find anything. That way I can tell Der—" He stopped himself. "Yes. Let's go through your locker."

Der—? Derby? Why did Mr. Stanley have to prove something about me to Edward Derby? More than ever, I was going to expose that man as a con artist.

We walked slowly down the hallway. The faint hum of busy classrooms reached us from various doors along the way.

It didn't take me long to open the combination lock. When the locker swung open, I was glad that I had cleaned out two months of lunch leftovers the week before.

"Here you are, Mr. Stanley. I don't mind if you go through anything in there."

He pointed to the marble bag on the top shelf.

"I'll start with that."

I grabbed it and handed it to him. He loosened the strings with his right hand and poured marbles into the huge palm of his left hand.

As he did that, I started pulling things out of my locker. A busted calculator. The spare hat I wore as often as possible to hide my current haircut. A pair of extra sneakers for Mike. Three jackets. A book called *The Adventures of Tom Sawyer*. Another book called—

"Ricky."

The deadliness of his tone hit me like a punch.

I turned slowly as Mr. Stanley lowered his open palm.

I stared at the assortment of marbles. And nearly fainted.

Crisp and cool. Four diamonds glittered crisp and cool among the marbles across the skin of his palm.

CHAPTER  15

It's hard to think quickly when you're on the verge of throwing up, passing out, and running away all at the same time.

So I breathed as deep as I could and struggled for words. Without success. Mr. Stanley broke the silence first.

"I believe this is a criminal matter," he said very quietly. "Come to the office. We'll call your parents from there."

"Sir, there must be another explanation."

"Really?" he asked with a deadly arch of his eyebrows. "You've got thirty seconds to come up with it."

Mr. Stanley spun on his heels and didn't wait for me to follow.

My mind whirred as I trailed him to the office. *Joel had those marbles last. Mrs. McEwan will never let me work at her house again. My debt will never be repaid. I'll be sent to a delinquency school. Joel had those marbles last. Joel had those marbles last. Joel had those marbles last.*

Those were the words I blurted out as soon as Mr. Stanley closed the office door behind us and stared down at me with a mixture of pity, scorn, and anger.

"Joel had those marbles last."

"That is pretty low, Ricky." He spat the words at me, "You're blaming a defenseless six-year-old kid. Worse, you're blaming a six-year-old kid who thinks the sun sets on you."

The implications of my words hit me. Suddenly I knew how the diamonds had made it into the marble bag.

"I didn't say he was the thief, sir, I said he had them *last*. Somebody else was the thief, and it wasn't me!"

Only I didn't know if I had a way of proving it. Yet the excitement in my voice reached past Mr. Stanley's anger.

"Okay," he said. "You've got one shot. Make it good."

I took a deep breath.

"Would you please call Joel and his teacher here into the office?"

"That's not much of a shot, Ricky. Give me a reason why I should."

I looked Mr. Stanley straight in the eye. "Because my whole future rests on being proven innocent."

He stared back at me for several long seconds. "I won't call them here. We'll go to them instead," he finally announced.

The school corridor seemed like one of those terrible tunnels you sometimes face in a dream. Dark and foggy and stretching for forever as something chases you while your feet move in slow motion.

My fear wasn't a fear of being wrong. I knew, of course, that I hadn't stolen the diamonds. My fear was that I couldn't prove it. And it all rested on Joel.

We stopped in front of his classroom door. The smell of

Elmer's glue hit us. Mrs. Quinn, Joel's teacher, answered our knock. She had scissors in her hand, a cut-out paper cat stuck to her chin, and a sparkle in her eye.

"Why, hello," she said.

"Hello, Shirley. I'm sorry to interrupt," Mr. Stanley said. "But Ricky here has a question for you."

I tried not to stare at the paper cat on her chin. "Yes, ma'am. Do you remember if you let Joel, my brother, out for a bathroom break yesterday morning around ten-thirty?"

She thought for a moment. "Why, yes, as a matter of fact, I did."

My shoulders sagged with relief. Half the battle was won. That's when the commotion had taken place.

"Although that's a significant time, that doesn't prove anything," Mr. Stanley said to me.

Mrs. Quinn swung her head back to face Mr. Stanley. The paper cat quivered on her chin. "Is Joel in trouble?"

"No," I said before he could answer. "I am. But if I could borrow him briefly, I might not be."

"If it's fine with Mr. Stanley, it's fine with me," she said.

He nodded, but then reached out and held her shoulder as she turned to go back inside the classroom. "Shirley," he said gently, "before you go back, you should know there is something stuck to your chin."

She giggled. "Of course there is. The six year olds think it's a funny accident, so they stare when they think I'm not looking. The best part is they believe that if they stay real quiet I won't notice it's there. Much easier than shushing them every two minutes."

With that, she bustled back inside.

"What a woman," Mr. Stanley said admiringly. "She— *eeeep!*"

I'm glad I'm not the only person who jumps when Joel makes his sudden appearances.

Joel looked up at us with inquiring eyes.

Before Mr. Stanley could say a word, I spoke.

"Sir, could you show him the diamonds?"

Mr. Stanley frowned a puzzled frown, but reached for the handkerchief he had used to wrap the diamonds, hesitated briefly, then held them out for Joel to see.

Joel smiled. "Pretty. Same as mine."

"The ones you gave me in your marble bag, right?"

"In your locker," Joel said. "Safe."

My heart burst with relief. Joel still thought his marble bag was safe in my locker.

Startled, Mr. Stanley glanced at me. I gave a slight warning shake of the head. I now had to clear Joel of the theft.

"Where did you find the pretty stones?" I said to Joel. "Can you show us?"

Joel considered the request gravely, then nodded.

I whispered to Mr. Stanley, "Give him a head start, sir."

Joel slipped forward. He seemed to glide down the waxed floors of the hallways. I realized for the millionth time how much of a ghost he can be. I also realized it was exactly why he had managed to get the diamonds the day before. Mr. Stanley and I followed, elephants trying to keep up to a fox.

Joel rounded one corner, slipped down the hallway to another corner, and disappeared. When we reached that corner, we saw Joel on his tiptoes in front of a glass case that held a length of folded emergency fire hose.

As we watched, Joel reached up and rapped on the glass door. It popped open. Then he began fishing underneath the fire hose. He continued fishing earnestly until we arrived beside him.

"They were here," he announced. "But there aren't any more."

Wordlessly he pushed his way between Mr. Stanley and me and scooted back down the hallway. I didn't blame him. A paper cat on your teacher's chin is much more interesting than the search for one or two more pretty stones.

Mr. Stanley spoke slowly. "I'm prepared to admit you didn't steal those diamonds, Ricky. And that none of your friends did, either. I'm also prepared to admit that you had no way of knowing they would be stored in your locker. But beyond that, I'm baffled."

I took a deep breath, Because now *I* would be making a terrible accusation. "Sir, consider for a moment that Edward Derby stole those diamonds. After all, he was at the front of the room during the snake stampede."

Mr. Stanley's jaw dropped. "Not possible. He was the first one we searched in the classroom yesterday. In fact, he insisted we search him."

I said, "He was also the only person to leave the room before the search began. Remember, he went to your office to call you back. What if along the way he stopped here and—"

Bingo. Mr. Stanley's eyes shot wide open. His pale scalp also began to redden with anger. "The nerve of that man! The sheer nerve. That means all he needed to do on the way to the office was to find a safe hiding place for the diamonds."

"Exactly," I said. "He thought he could return at his leisure later to collect them. Except he had the bad luck of stashing them while Joel was prowling the hallways. Joel, of course, stopped by later to see what the man had been doing in the fire hose case. And discovered the pretty stones, which he stored in the marble bag."

"It makes sense," Mr. Stanley said. He sighed. "Too much sense. I suppose I should call the police."

"Um, sir," I said, thinking of how badly I wanted to expose Edward Derby as an impostor. "Maybe we could wait on that."

"But the man's a thief."

"It's his word against Joel's, *if* Joel even feels like talking. And who would the police believe?"

Mr. Stanley rubbed his chin. "It's too bad we couldn't put substitute diamonds underneath the fire hose and catch

Derby with them. I don't dare leave the real ones there."

I was thinking of how long Sergeant Brotsky had said it would take for the fingerprint results to be returned. "Could you wait a few days before reporting to Mrs. McEwan that you have found her diamonds?" I asked. "Maybe until Monday?"

Mr. Stanley studied my face, then nodded.

CHAPTER 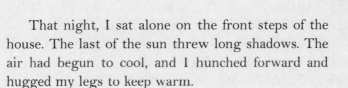 16

That night, I sat alone on the front steps of the house. The last of the sun threw long shadows. The air had begun to cool, and I hunched forward and hugged my legs to keep warm.

"Hey." It was my dad's gentle voice as he sat beside me.

"Hey," I said back without a lot of enthusiasm.

"Life's got you down, huh."

I nodded. He didn't ask for details. Dad was good like that. He knew if I wanted to talk, I would.

"When you were only a couple of years old," he said, "there were times when we were walking together and you would reach up and hold my hand and we'd get to wherever I was taking you."

I turned my head, half frowning. *Where was this coming from?*

"It made me feel so special," Dad said. "Even though you could talk by then, you never asked where we were going. You never asked if it would be a long walk or a short walk. You never asked if it would be dangerous or boring or fun. You just reached up and took my hand and stayed with me."

I couldn't help but smile as I pictured a little kid walking with his dad.

"It made me feel special because you trusted me com-pletely," Dad continued. "You didn't worry at all, because you knew you were with me and I would take care of you."

He let that hang until I broke the silence.

"This has a point, right?" I said, knowing he was waiting for me to speak.

"There is so little about life that you can control," he said. "You can control how you choose to face what happens, and you can control your own actions, but beyond that . . ."

He paused. "Here's the point. Most people will tell you that it hurts God when you do something like steal or lie. And it's true. God's like a father. He's hurt partly because it's wrong, and partly because He knows that those actions hurt you, and He doesn't like seeing you hurt. The same way that Mom and I don't like to see you hurt."

"Yes," I said. "I can see that."

"I think it hurts God just as much when you worry," Dad said quietly. "Jesus said that very plainly. Worrying doesn't change the future at all. Worrying is like saying to God that you don't trust Him. Just like I would have been hurt when you were little and you didn't trust me enough to hold my hand when we walked."

He stood and patted my shoulder. "Ask for help if you need it. Take whatever positive actions you can to change troublesome situations. But don't waste energy on worry. God is in control, son, even when you can't see the big picture and understand all of what's happening around you."

I thought about it for a moment.

"Thanks, Dad," I said. And meant it.

He left me there alone. And quiet. And feeling much less anxious.

The next day in school was no different than the first part of the week. During both of those days Mike and Ralphy ignored me to talk to small groups of people in mysterious whispers.

I barely cared. The clock was ticking down much too quickly on the remaining few days left to find definite proof that Edward Derby was a con artist trying to steal from Mrs. McEwan. Sergeant Brotsky had had no word for me on Wednesday after school. After my stop at the police station on Thursday—still no word on Edward Derby's real identity—I went directly to Mrs. McEwan's house and knocked at the back door.

She let me in. I hurried through the porch. Her earrings sparkled discreetly in the late afternoon sunlight.

She looked at me oddly. "Where are you headed in such a rush?"

"Upstairs," I told her, almost feeling guilty because I wanted any clues to prove Edward Derby was a con artist. "I wanted to check how the room looks. That is, the room I've been painting."

"Yes. Of course."

Still, she looked at me oddly. Then, as if making a sudden decision, she sat down and motioned for me to sit beside her at the kitchen table.

She patted the top of my hand.

"Ricky," she began slowly, "I've known you for quite some time. I've watched you grow up. You've helped me here a lot in the last year and a half. And I'm quite fond of you."

She then looked past me, out the kitchen window at the tips of the large oak trees swaying in the spring breeze. For a moment she seemed tired and old, as if she were trying to gather strength. So I waited.

"I really don't want to talk about this," she began again.

"Yet on the other hand, I cannot bear to wonder much longer. It's about the jewelry collection. Promise you won't be hurt by the questions I must ask you."

Her voice had become sad, matching that shift of age in her face. What could she be trying to say? Was she, too, beginning to suspect me? But why? I decided to wait for her questions before defending myself. "I'll do the best I can," I said.

"Thank you. I need to ask because some strange things have been happening around here and—"

The screen door clicked as somebody else walked into the back porch. I sat out of sight of the doorway, so I didn't know who had entered. I only heard his voice.

"I was just at the school," Edward Derby said from the porch as he stamped his shoes clean. "They say they're doing their best to find the diamonds, but you already know what I think about the situation. How you ever managed to trust that k—"

"Edward," Mrs. McEwan smiled at me as she made her voice carry across the kitchen to him. "Ricky's arrived. He's sitting here about to hear my grocery list. That, of course, will save you a trip to the store."

Grocery list? Grocery list? I almost sighed with relief. She got me all worked up about difficult questions and strange happenings just to ease me into the job of going to the grocery store? And grown-ups think kids are weird.

There was sudden silence from the porch.

Finally Edward entered the kitchen. "As I was saying," he finally said. "How you ever managed to trust the safety of that collection"—he emphasized the *k* sound of *collection*—"in a public place like a school is something I will never understand."

Derby smiled at me briefly and without interest, then continued walking. "I'll be upstairs if you need me." He paused. "Aunt Jane."

Inside, I seethed. *I* knew full well why he had to remind himself to call her "Aunt." But could I convince Mrs. McEwan?

Derby's footsteps finished their quiet clicks up the staircase.

"You were saying something, Mrs. McEwan?" I asked in the silence.

She shook her head as if to clear it. There was no trace of sadness when she spoke again. "Oh yes. Silly me. I was going to ask if you minded going to the grocery store right now. Friday's the day Mrs. Ghettley usually stops in for afternoon coffee and cake. She's such a poor old dear, I don't want to disappoint her tomorrow by not having anything on hand."

"Sure," I said. "But what about the questions you wanted to ask?"

"Oh, those," she said. "They're certainly not so important that they can't wait."

Things were getting stranger by the minute. I was ready to regret I had ever seen the Jewel of Madagascar.

It took roughly ten minutes for Mrs. McEwan to assemble her list for me. She promised my grocery shopping time would give me an hour's worth of credit toward paying back my debt.

As I walked down the street, I did the math. After this, it only left me eighteen hours of work to go. That meant I could be out of debt by—

Edward Derby!

Yes! Edward Derby! I was barely out of the house and there he was. A hundred yards ahead of me and striding quickly down the sidewalk!

How had he done it? I had been in the kitchen the whole time. How had he left the house without me seeing him?

It didn't matter. He had to be followed.

I tried putting into practice the opposite of everything I had learned from years of trying to avoid Joel's uncanny ability to follow me.

It worked.

I snuck around trees, behind cars, under fences, and between hedges. I followed him as far as the nearest phone booth.

And that's all he did. Was phone.

I crept behind a car, leaned on a bumper, poked my head around the edge of the fender, and watched.

He punched in numbers. I counted. Eleven touch-tone numbers. It didn't take a genius to realize that it meant the number "one," then three area code digits, and a regular seven-digit phone number. *Who was he calling long distance? Why did he have to leave the house to do it?*

My knees began to cramp, but I was determined to wait it out.

Three things happened at once.

Joel sneezed behind me, which nearly scared the fingernails right off my hands. The car in front of me suddenly started up. And Edward Derby stared in amazement as I fell from the bumper as the car pulled away from me.

I dusted myself off and, glad that at least he was with me to make it look less suspicious, I reached back for Joel. Thin air. Naturally.

I coughed a few times and left for the grocery store with as much dignity as I could muster. Which put me in a bad mood that stayed, especially as I met Mike, my former best friend, leaving the grocery store.

"Um, hi," he said with a mouthful of red licorice.

"Hi," I said. Then, knowing that I shouldn't give up so easily on him, I decided to at least try to be friendly. "What's up?"

He looked around. "Nothing. Absolutely nothing."

"Oh," I said. "What's in the bag?"

He pulled it back and hid it under his shirt. "A present for my mom."

"That's nice," I said. There was no way I was going to betray the sudden pain I felt at his lie. Nobody buys their mom red licorice for a present, which was obviously what he carried in the bag.

"See you later," he said, breaking into a run.

"Yeah," I said, and turned around, only to bump into Ralphy.

"Gotta run," he spit out from the grocery store entrance. He, too, cradled a small, full bag between his hands. Bits of red licorice clung to his front teeth.

I sighed in frustration.

Edward Derby, friends who were strangers, it was all happening too quickly for me. I took a deep breath, closed my eyes briefly, then pushed ahead to get the grocery shopping list for Mrs. Ghettley's Friday afternoon visit.

And, to end a completely weird afternoon, when I went to buy some red licorice of my own, it was gone. All of it gone, except for one skinny, sickly looking red-licorice worm.

Wonderful.

It took me until I was halfway home to realize what that meant.

Mike's words from the day before ran through my mind. *"I'll fool everybody in town,"* Mike had said to Ralphy by the lockers. *"They'll think I'm eating real worms."*

Michael S. Andrews, former best friend of Ricky L. Kidd, was up to a major trick. Without me to help.

I decided I would find a way to mess him up. Without him knowing it.

CHAPTER 17

I can safely say nothing happened Friday. That is, if having everybody around you in school look at you and whisper and giggle is nothing happening. I didn't want to believe the Jewel of Madagascar had cursed me. But by the end of the day, I could see no other explanation.

Worse, I made no progress on the Edward Derby situation. After school I followed him for twenty minutes. Ten minutes as he wheeled Mrs. Ghettley home from Mrs. McEwan's after their coffee party. And ten minutes as he strolled back again.

There wasn't much time left until the Monday deadline.

During breakfast on Saturday, I received a phone call from Mike.

"Hey, Ricky! Meet me at the library in half an hour?"

Suddenly the sourness in me that had been stewing

over the past week disappeared. I was glad to hear from him. Still, I was cautious.

"Any reason?"

"Sure. But it's a surprise."

"Does it have anything to do with the way you and Ralphy have been acting this week?" I asked.

Mike laughed. "I guess you noticed. Yes, it does. You'll find out all about it, pal."

I felt terrific as I hung up the phone. Whatever had been wrong all week would soon be fixed. I would tell him all my worries and fears about Edward Derby. It would be a great relief not to be alone with my troubles. Mike, my buddy and friend, and Ralphy, my buddy and friend, would be there to help me through this.

I left immediately, not bothering to shake Joel as he followed me.

Strangely enough, streams of people were moving down the sidewalks toward and past me as I headed down to the library. I felt like a fish battling the current. Even stranger, they seemed to be staring at me, but whenever I looked at them, they quickly dropped their eyes.

Was it my imagination? Were all these people talking about me? Because whenever they came within hello distance, their voices dropped to whispers.

And where were they going? The only thing behind me in the direction they were going was the school.

I was ready to go crazy.

After waiting for ten minutes at the library, I called Mike's house. Not home. At the school, his mom told me.

My blood boiled.

So everything would be better? Fat chance. Mike had lied.

I fumed for several minutes, debating my choices for the morning. Should I go to Mrs. McEwan's house and wait to follow Edward Derby? Or should I go to the school and tell

Mike and Ralphy that our friendship was through?

The bitter taste in my mouth told me to go to the school.

Dozens of people were lined up at the entrance to the school. Above a doorway a large hand-painted sign read: *THE GREAT MIKE ANDREWS WORM-EATING CARNIVAL.*

I marched to the school ready to throttle my former friends.

Ralphy separated himself from a group of people. He was carrying a large paper bag. His grin stretched wide across his skinny face.

"Ricky! Your timing is perfect! We didn't want you here any earlier."

"Obviously," I said.

Ralphy took my arm and pulled me around the side of the school where nobody could see us.

"You have a new name for the morning," he said, still beaming. "Here. Put this on. And call yourself—" he paused for importance—"the Renowned Ricky."

"Huh?"

He thrust a bed sheet into my hands. And a string of big fake pearls. And a purple turban.

Ralphy laughed with delight at my confusion. "We fooled you, didn't we? This is a total surprise for you, isn't it?! That's why we sent you to the library while we got set up this morning. To keep this secret as long as possible."

"Huh?"

He chortled more. "Quick. Put all that on. You're going to be a genius."

"Huh?"

"This is too good. This is too good," he said between giggles.

Ralphy stepped back to watch my face. "This is a fund-raiser," he said, pausing between each word. "A fund-raiser for Ricky Kidd!"

"All this secrecy a fund-raiser for me?" My knees began to buckle as the shame of doubting my friends overwhelmed me. "Why?"

"Why else?" Ralphy said with a grin. "Because of that accident with the jewelry. You didn't think we'd let you struggle alone to pay it back, did you? Wait here for a second."

He spun on his heels and ran back to the school entrance.

I stood in a complete daze, holding the bedsheet, turban, and pearls.

Ralphy returned with Mike and said, "Mike can explain. It was his idea."

Mike's cap was on backward, and his grin was pure joy. "We don't have much time before the carnival begins, and we need your help in the Genius Booth. I'll try to explain quickly."

I still didn't move. Not even a twitch.

"I had it planned for tonight," Mike grinned. "But then I found out about Mom's birthday party tonight. So I changed it to morning and told everybody the early bird gets the worm."

"Worm?" I asked.

"Remember the worm throwing we did in your backyard? Ralphy here was so fascinated by it that he forgot to put his shirt on before chasing me. In fact, he forgot that his chest was bare until Lisa reminded him. And we both know how shy Ralphy is about his chest."

Ralphy blushed.

"Anyway," Mike continued, "when we were eating cookies—just before you were attacked by that spider—I realized that people would love to watch a worm-eating contest. Then

I realized they would love even more to be part of one. That is, as long as they were doing the throwing and not the eating."

Although I was numb with bewilderment, I nodded.

"So who better to be a target than me, Mike Andrews?" he asked. "People in this town have a long memory, and once or twice in the past I've played tricks around here. I figured they'd love a chance to get me back."

That part was very true. Not that people dislike Mike and want to do bad things to him. Just the opposite. People liked him as much as anybody in town. He's the kind of guy who brightens your day with his grin, even if he has just played a good trick on you. And just about everybody in Jamesville has had their day brightened by him for both reasons. Mike also grins just as big when you play a joke on him. He figures if you outsmart him, you deserve the fun, even if it takes him a minute or two to see the humor in it.

I nodded again.

"So," Ralphy said. "He came up with The Great Mike Andrews Worm-Eating Carnival. All the kids in our class agreed to help by setting up contest booths. Admission to the carnival is fifty cents, and people pay extra to enter each contest. The prizes at each booth are worm-throwing tickets. Because at the end of the carnival, people can cash those tickets in to try throwing worms in Mike's mouth. Whatever lands inside, he eats."

"Except," Mike interrupted, "they won't know I'm not eating real worms!" He dropped his voice to a whisper. "It's the best trick I've played on anybody yet. I'll be eating licorice worms!"

"Yes! Yes!" Ralphy said. "That was my idea. Mike was prepared to eat real worms because you were so worried about the money you needed to pay Mrs. McEwan. But I came up with a plan."

"Oh?" I said despite the lump in my stomach.

"Yup. Red Jell-O cubes. We cut up the licorice worms and put the pieces in liquid Jell-O. After it set, we made cubes. It makes the worms look like the real thing. And Jell-O cubes are easier to throw than dangly old worms."

So much for the curse of the Jewel of Madagascar.

"You guys went to all this work for me?"

Mike stuck his hand out for me to shake it. "You bet, pal. Not many things are more important than friendship. Especially with you."

It didn't seem like a good moment to tell them why I felt so terrible.

CHAPTER 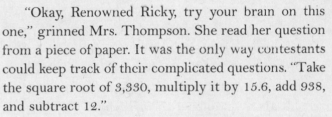 18

"Okay, Renowned Ricky, try your brain on this one," grinned Mrs. Thompson. She read her question from a piece of paper. It was the only way contestants could keep track of their complicated questions. "Take the square root of 3,330, multiply it by 15.6, add 938, and subtract 12."

A dozen people were in line behind her. All of them were waiting for my first mistake, ready to pay fifty cents for the chance to ask the question that would stump me.

The fund-raiser was a terrific idea, but I felt bad about it. How could I have doubted my friends? I didn't deserve their help and care. But being a genius in this booth wasn't giving me much time to dwell on how stupid I had been.

"Boy, that's a tough one," I said. I closed my eyes and frowned in concentration. I repeated slowly, "The square root of 3,330 times 15.6, plus 938, minus 12."

I squeezed my eyes shut to think hard, then opened them to thoughtfully stare at the floor.

"The answer is . . . 1,826.2159. Give or take a few ten-thousandths."

Mrs. Thompson wrote my answer down on the paper provided at my booth. Then she took the calculator—also provided.

"Wrong!" she said. "It's 2,285.65!" She rubbed her hands. "I believe you owe me one worm-eating ticket."

People behind her smiled in satisfaction.

"It was a tough question, Mrs. Thompson," I said. "Would you mind running it through the calculator again?"

"Are you saying I made the mistake?"

That started them whispering behind her.

"Please, ma'am?" I asked respectfully. And gravely. After all, a mathematical genius wearing a purple turban—which nicely hid the aftermath of a Breton haircut—has to keep his dignity.

She punched numbers back into the calculator. "The square root of 3,330—multiplied by 15.6—plus 938—minus 12—equals—"

"It's beyond belief," she gasped. "It does equal 1,862.2159. I must have hit a wrong number the first time."

That set the lineup of people buzzing.

I shrugged modestly. "Would you like to try again?"

Mrs. Thompson grinned from beneath her flowered hat. "You bet your turban, baby." She plunked down two quarters and scribbled down another question.

"1,289 divided by 76.3, multiplied by the square root of 12,883."

"Hmmm." I stared thoughtfully at the floor in front of me again. "1,917.5066."

She held her breath while pressing the calculator buttons. "You're right again! How do you do it?"

I looked at all the people behind her. Then I leaned forward to whisper the secret in her ear.

She leaned forward and nearly drove a flower from her hat into my eye. "Cheerios," I told her. "I eat lots of Cheerios. They're good for the brain."

She giggled as she walked to another booth.

The hand-painted sign above my makeshift booth read:

Fool the Renowned Ricky and win a worm-throwing ticket.

We were in the school gym with booths all around us. By the laughing and hum of other people noises, it sounded like the carnival was busy and fun and successful. My guess was that over sixty people had come to try their luck at winning chances to make Mike Andrews eat worms.

Some of the popular booths were the two BB-gun-target-shooting booths, the dart-throwing-balloon booth where the balloons had small tags inside with the prize you could win, and the ring-tossing booth.

Hit the targets and win worm-throwing tickets, the sign said.

But the carnival didn't stop there. One kid in our class had rigged a stiff wire between two small posts. The wire wasn't straight, though. It curved up and down like hills and valleys, and it was hooked to a small red light and a buzzer. The trick was to test your steadiness by moving a tiny loop from one post to the other without letting it touch the wire. If the loop touched, an electrical circuit was completed, and the light went on and the buzzer sounded.

Three buzzes or fewer and win a worm-throwing ticket.

There was a Trivial Pursuit booth, where people could choose from multiple choice answers to weird questions.

Get four out of five answers right and win a worm-throwing ticket.

All together, there were fifteen booths. As I looked around and enjoyed the carnival atmosphere, a part of me felt warm for having a group of people pitch in together to help me out of my debt. Even the grown-ups who were spending the money were all trying to help.

On the other hand, a big part of me inside felt as if it had been slugged with a baseball bat. I had been so prepared to hate all these people, so prepared to be angry and bitter, so prepared to be alone. My trust in friendship had not been able to stand much, I told myself. It was a lesson I vowed never to forget.

And I realized that showing sadness now would ruin it for the people who were enjoying trying to help me. I would put on a brave front and save my sadness for later when I asked my friends for forgiveness.

So the Renowned Ricky tried to smile mysteriously.

I would have stayed renowned for a lot longer, except for one thing: Joel unplugged me.

If Joel were a computer, his main program would read: Foil Ricky. Almost as if Mom and Dad, to keep track of me, had ordered an extra pair of eyes.

Anyway, the answers were rolling smoothly and easily, no matter how complicated the question. I'd close my eyes in concentration, open them, look down thoughtfully, and come up with the answer.

Everybody was amazed.

They shouldn't have been. Ralphy was underneath the cloth-covered table that served as the front of the booth. He had the keyboard of his iMac on his lap. The monitor, attached to the keyboard by its stretched-out cord, was at my feet, tilted upward. For me, it was a simple matter of looking down and frowning in concentration as Ralphy punched in the mathematics and put the answer in front of me.

Simple and foolproof. But not Joelproof.

I noticed him at the side. He was standing on the electrical cord that led to our booth. And frowning to himself, curious about the cord.

The Renowned Ricky is supposed to remain cool under any circumstances. What could I do? Ask Joel to leave? With all those people lined up in front of me? Right. They'd wonder why Joel made me nervous.

Instead, I did nothing. Fortunately, nobody else noticed Joel. He put his teddy bear down and dropped to his knees to look under the edge of the tablecloth that nearly reached the floor.

Great.

If anybody else decided to look, our game was over.

Joel waved at Ralphy. The only thing I can figure is that Ralphy didn't wave back and Joel wanted his attention. So Joel followed the electrical cord to the wall and unplugged it. He crawled back to the table, still holding the end of the cord, and disappeared under the cloth to join Ralphy.

Nobody had noticed him crawling around. Which didn't surprise me.

When the end of the cord made it as far underneath as Ralphy, I heard a small moan from behind the cloth. Which didn't surprise me, either.

Mr. Evans, my teacher, missed Ralphy's moan. He was still having trouble with his new hearing aid.

"—end of the year, Ricky?"

"I'm sorry, Mr. Evans. Could you repeat the question?" The sick feeling from betraying my friends during the very time they were nobly helping me only increased as I glanced at the blank monitor.

"It wasn't my question yet," he said. "I just want you to know how proud I am of you. Even though I've taught you nearly all year, I had no idea you verged on genius in mathematics."

"It's nothing," I said truthfully, ready to faint.

"Give me the square root of four hundred, multiplied by twenty," Mr. Evans said.

"The square root of four hundred, multiplied by twenty," I repeated. I don't know why. Even though Ralphy could hear me, he had no way of plugging the figures into his computer keyboard. No power. Lots of Joel, but no power.

"Good question," I said. I was ready to give up, but I looked at the ground anyway.

Suddenly Ralphy's hand shot into sight! It was frantically waving four fingers!

What could it mean? How could four be the answer? His hand waved harder as I waited. If his fingers had been helicopter blades, his hand would have taken off. I didn't like it, but if Ralphy insisted—

"Four?"

The hand slumped to the ground.

Mr. Evans frowned and sighed.

"That's a ridiculous guess, Ricky. Not even close," he said. "The square root of four hundred is twenty. So if you multiply it by twenty, you have what you started with. A simple trick question. Get it? A simple trick question."

"Good one, Mr. Evans," I said.

He shook his head as he walked away with a worm-eating ticket.

He had been the last of the lineup. Because temporarily there was nothing for me to do, my misery pressed on me. Would my friends forgive me for doubting them? I felt more miserable as I looked over at Mike. Sweet Mike, who had been willing to eat real worms to help me.

He was pacing in his corner of the gym.

Behind him, in all readiness, was the crowning spectacle of the carnival, the worm-eating booth. It was a stepladder, covered bottom to top with dazzling red crepe paper. Under the ladder was a large plastic sheet to keep the hardwood floor clean of Jell-O and worms. Behind the ladder, against the wall, was another plastic sheet to keep Jell-O cubes from squashing against the bricks. Twenty feet in front of the ladder was a table draped with fancy white sheets. And beside the table was a set of drums.

Then beyond Mike, I saw something that froze me.

Half hidden by a high pile of gym mats, the far door of the gym had been propped open to let the fresh spring breeze inside.

Edward Derby was trying to wheel Mrs. Ghettley through that door. As they went through the doorway, Mrs. Ghettley spread her arms wide to push against the walls and stop the motion of the wheelchair.

Edward Derby quickly looked to see if anyone was observing, then slapped the poor old woman's arms down with a roughness that made me wince.

She struggled briefly, but it was no use.

He wheeled her out of my sight.

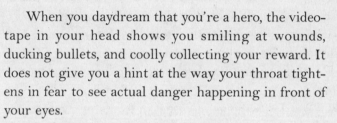

CHAPTER 19

When you daydream that you're a hero, the video-tape in your head shows you smiling at wounds, ducking bullets, and coolly collecting your reward. It does not give you a hint at the way your throat tightens in fear to see actual danger happening in front of your eyes.

I had managed to stammer an excuse at the booth and begin to walk as quickly as I could toward the direction that Edward Derby had kidnapped Mrs. Ghettley in her wheelchair. I had plunged ahead, alone, with my heart hammering in excitement at the chase. I had reached Mrs. McEwan's house in time to see the two of them rounding the narrow sidewalk that led to the backyard. I had run the entire time without thinking.

And when, on hands and knees, I slowly peeked around the corner of the house, to actually see it happening—instead of viewing it as a scene on television—made my throat tighten with fear.

Edward Derby, his back to me, was tying Mrs. Ghettley to her wheelchair!

A small part of my brain detached itself to think over my odds. Edward Derby was a big man, obviously intent on hurting someone. If I marched out and told him to quit, he'd bash me over the head and tie me alongside Mrs. Ghettley. What would happen next, I didn't want to imagine.

Think, Kidd, think!

Almost before I knew it, my hand was tightening over a weathered two-by-four board half leaning against the house beside me. It was the length of a baseball bat and had been used to prop some tomato vines higher into the sun.

Could I do it?

The thought of hitting someone across the head made me want to throw up. Yet who deserved it more than someone prepared to kidnap an old lady helpless in her wheelchair?

So I crept forward, wanting to hurry before he finished with the ropes, yet scared to make a noise. Step by half step, I moved forward until I was close enough to hear Derby's breathing.

Mrs. Ghettley, wrapped as usual in layers of shawls, suddenly looked up and her eyes shot wide with surprise. Because of that, Derby swung his head around just as I was raising the board.

"What the—"

His sudden movement gave me no time to think. I swung and swung hard, hoping even as the board came down that it wouldn't hurt him too badly.

The wood caught him just behind the ear. With a small moan, he collapsed.

I let out a deep breath.

"It's okay, Mrs. Ghettley. He won't hurt you now."

She mumbled. "Oh dear. The nice man said he was taking me on a car ride."

"Not with ropes, he wasn't," I said.

"Cowboys and Indians?" she asked hopefully.

As I untied Mrs. Ghettley, the relief of having all my worries over made me giddy. Working the rope loose near her wrists, I nearly giggled again at her garish red nail polish.

Edward Derby moaned.

Poetic justice, I thought, with the rope still in my hands. *I'll tie him with his own rope.*

"Mrs. Ghettley," I said, "this will just take a second. Then I'll take you back to the gym."

"Such a nice spring day," she said. "And you remind me a lot of a boy I know. His name is Ricky Kidd. But he never wears a hat quite like yours."

"That's me." I tried to explain the turban, but then quit. There was no use in it.

I turned and began pushing Edward Derby's heavy body into position. I tied the knots quickly and tightly, not knowing how much time remained before he would regain consciousness.

As I finished the last of the knots, I heard a slight scraping sound behind me.

Then a thunderclap exploded at the back of my head. Blackness hit me just as my face slammed into the ground.

"Ricky, are you okay?"

Walls swam in front of my eyes. I was dreaming that Lisa Higgins' voice was calling me at the bottom of a dark, dark swimming pool.

"Speak to me, Ricky! Tell me you're okay!"

"Sure," I mumbled. "This water's weird. You can breathe it."

A great light shone into the dark water, and I struggled to reach the surface. But my arms would not move.

"There's no water here, Ricky. Open your eyes."

I did. My head felt like mashed watermelon. Then I focused.

I was in Mrs. McEwan's basement. I recognized it by the paintings and the Victorian decorations around me. Yet I was still dreaming. A section of the wall was wide open, showing a dark cave.

I blinked.

And looked down.

My arms were pinned to a chair by rope. I felt something warm against the back of my shoulders.

"Lisa?" Things became clearer. She was tied to a chair behind me, her back against mine.

"Yes," she said with relief. "I thought you were—that you were—"

I knew she wanted to say "dead," so I broke in, "You thought I was pretending this was math class, right?"

She laughed, but softly and only for a moment.

"Not too loudly," she warned. "He's returning."

It started coming back. Edward Derby. Mrs. Ghettley. And a blow to my head.

"He?"

"The terrible man who was dragging you into the house."

"You've never seen him before?"

"Yes," she said, "but I can't remember where. Ralphy told me to follow you because it was funny the way you left the carnival. He couldn't leave the Genius Booth, and of course Mike is getting ready for the worm eating. I ran around the corner just as that man was dragging you, and by then it was too late. He caught me and tied me down here with you."

I half shook my head to clear it more, but stopped quickly at the intense throbbing pain.

"Edward Derby? And Mrs. Ghettley?"

"Derby was on the ground. Tied with rope. Mrs. Ghettley was gone, Ricky. One handle of her wheelchair bent downward and some shawls left on the seat. Nothing else."

How long had I been unconscious? Long enough, I guessed, for the stranger to get rid of Mrs. Ghettley before coming back to do the same to me. A thought that had been bothering me came back.

I struggled at the ropes, "Lisa! You said *he* would return. How do you know?"

She spoke very quietly. "The same reason I know why that man did all this."

My mind wasn't tracking properly.

Lisa continued in that same quiet voice. "Look to your right, Ricky."

In a velvet-lined box were sparkly jewels, still bright in the dim light of the basement.

"Mrs. McEwan's collection!"

"Yes," came the reply. But not from Lisa.

The voice came from the darkness where that section of the wall had been opened.

A man stepped through! He wore rough, dark working clothes and a pair of gloves.

"You," I blurted, recognizing him instantly. "You're John Davies. The gardener Mrs. McEwan fired a year and a half ago!"

"Not that remembering will do you any good, kid. By the time anyone finds you here, I'll be long gone." He smirked. "With the jewelry."

CHAPTER 20

It always kills me when guys in movies yell, "You'll never get away with this!" even though they're helpless and about to be run over by a train or something like that.

So I didn't say anything to John Davies. I was tied up. He wasn't.

Lisa said it instead. As she called him a creep.

Davies held a knife out and laughed. The evil rang through his voice. "Unless there's a ghost around to help you untie those knots, I'll get away with anything I want." He stopped suddenly and snarled coldly, "Besides. You don't want to stop me. After what I've gone through to get this far, I'll kill to protect this jewelry. Even you."

He grabbed the box and tucked it under his arm.

"Wait!" I said.

Incredibly enough, he did.

"That, that"—I motioned at the hole in the wall with my head—"what is that?"

"A secret passageway, stupid. Don't they teach you nothing in school?"

I ignored the insult—and the bad grammar. "With stairs and everything?"

He shook his head impatiently. "Of course with

stairs and everything. What good is a secret passageway unless it goes all over a house?"

"But how did you—"

"Question period is over, kid." He waggled his knife at us, smirked again, walked into the opening, and closed the door behind him.

"Nuts," I said. "All he has to do is revive Edward Derby, and they're both gone with Mrs. McEwan's entire fortune in jewels."

"Edward Derby?" Lisa asked from behind me. "He's in on this, too?"

I explained everything, right down to tying him up. "Of course," I said, "there was no way I could know that John Davies was his partner. So I got walloped on the head by him when my back was turned. I sure hope Mrs. Ghettley is okay."

There was silence as we both struggled and pulled at our knots. Her shoulders felt warm against mine.

"Lisa," I said, eyeing a sword on the far wall. "Maybe if we can hop together, we can make it to that sword. We'll cut ourselves free."

"Good plan."

We managed three hops. On the fourth hop, I accidentally jammed my foot under a leg of my chair. We stumbled, then toppled onto our sides.

"Um, sorry, Lisa," I mumbled with my cheek pressed against the floor. "I guess it's not my day."

"Don't worry." She tried to be brave. "At least we're still alive."

We lay there on our sides for several minutes. There was no way we would make it onto our feet again, and I had no desire to kick helplessly against the air like a beetle stuck on its back.

In other words, we were in trouble.

"What if he comes back?" Lisa asked. "You know, like on

television where they have to get rid of anyone who can identify them?"

"Thanks, Lisa."

A fly landed on my cheek. I tried blowing at it from the
side of my mouth. It continued to stroll across my face. I
shook my head. The fly left, then settled on my nose. I shook
my head again. It landed again.

That did it. The frustration had been building for too
long. Breaking the jewels, being accused of being a thief at
school, waiting to catch Edward Derby, suspecting my
friends, having suspicion repaid with kindness by the worm-
eating carnival, catching Edward Derby, then having him and
his partner get away with the jewelry, falling while tied to a
chair, and now the final indignity. A stupid fly tap-dancing in
rhythm to the twitches of my nose.

"Prepare your ears," I said very calmly to Lisa.

"I beg your pardon?"

I replied at the top of my lungs. "Aaaaaaaaaaaaaaaaaaaaargh!"

When I finished, Lisa hissed, "Don't do that. He'll hear
you and—"

The door to the secret passageway creaked.

We had landed with our heads facing away from the
secret passage and could see nothing of the man's approach.
Suddenly the thought of a whole flock of flies on my nose
seemed like a nice alternative.

The door creaked farther. Stopped. Then squeaked again.
Stealthy footsteps approached. Then stopped. I was ready to
scream again, all my worst anger at John Davies for toying
with us.

He kept us in suspense for a minute that seemed longer
than the worst math test ever given.

One more footstep. It landed near the top of my head.
Then stopped.

Another dozen heartbeats of waiting. Still, I could see
nothing.

My heart pounded. And a teddy bear dropped on my face.

CHAPTER 21

Thanks to Joel and the teddy bear cavalry, we were untied within five minutes.

"How'd you find us?"

He pointed to a basement window. "Saw that funny man from there."

"Terrific, pal. Now we have to find the funny man," I said. "The fastest way is to call the police and alert them. Lisa, can you do that? And Joel—"

Nuts. He was gone again. I might have seen a flash of his leg as he slid into the secret passageway, but then again, maybe not.

I ran with Lisa up the stairs, grabbing my turban.

As she began dialing the number to the police, I shouted, "Tell Sergeant Brotsky there are two of them. John Davies and Edward Derby. I'm sure he knows them both by sight!"

Then I searched all the rooms of the main floor of the house. If Mrs. Ghettley wasn't outside, they might have left her behind inside. Of course, if they took her as a hostage, which was probably the original plan, the search was useless. At least, however, it couldn't be wasted time, because I was waiting anyway as Lisa finished explaining things to Sergeant Brotsky. And if they *had* left Mrs. Ghettley behind, I doubted they would have gone to the effort of lifting her to the second floor.

No sign of her.

"It's done!" Lisa shouted. "A couple of squad cars are out on the streets now."

As if answering us, we heard sirens in the distance. That, at least, would slow John Davies and Edward Derby down as they tried escaping town.

"Lisa," I said between puffing breaths, "there's not much more we can do here. Much as I hate it, we should head back to the gym and break the news to Mrs. McEwan."

When we arrived back, the carnival was a riot of noise and color. Nobody gave us a second glance, even though my turban, as Lisa pointed out much too late, was on backward.

Mike and Ralphy were at the far end of the gym, fiddling with the worm-eating booth. I would catch up to them later.

I dreaded approaching Mrs. McEwan with the awful news.

Lisa kept a reassuring hand on my elbow as we hurried through the crowd.

She gasped and squeezed my arm tight just as I called out to Mrs. McEwan.

"Look! She's safe! That's so wonderful!"

Suddenly my heart warmed, too. On the other side of Mrs. McEwan sat Mrs. Ghettley, wrapped in her shawls and comfortable in her wheelchair as she watched the dart-throwing booth with an absent smile on her face.

I didn't get it. Why had John Davies let her go? Mrs. Ghettley—I grinned thinking about her own little world—must have just wheeled herself back here like nothing had happened. Because to her, probably nothing had happened except for some "nice" man offering to take her for a car ride.

Lisa ran forward and hugged Mrs. Ghettley so hard that her old eyes opened wide with surprise, and she nearly fell out of her wheelchair.

Mrs. McEwan caught my eye.

"Ricky! You look flushed. And Lisa, why is she crying on Mrs. Ghettley?"

My words came out quickly. "Edward Derby. Kidnapped Mrs. Ghettley. John Davies. Your old gardener. Back again. Hit me after I hit Derby. Tied me up. Tied Lisa up. Joel untied us. Davies stole jewelry. Police now chasing Davies, Derby. Mrs. Ghettley now safe here."

I stopped to catch my breath.

Mrs. McEwan, despite my obvious panic to speak, smiled. "Slow down, Ricky. Start at the beginning."

By then Lisa had returned to my side.

Mrs. Ghettley, still smiling her absent smile, wheeled herself slowly to another booth.

Lisa took over for me as I struggled for composure. "I followed Ricky to your house, ma'am. When I got there, Edward Derby was tied up. I caught John Davies dragging Ricky into the house. He chased me down and tied us down in the basement together. Then used a secret passageway to escape. Joel untied us, but Davies has all your jewelry."

Mrs. McEwan's face sagged. "All my jewelry," she gasped. "That can't be. All I have left now is this—" Her voice trailed as she lifted her hand, palm downward, and extended her fingers. She looked forlornly at the remaining ring on her hand.

Something nagged. Where had I seen someone examining a hand earlier?

"Hold it," Mrs. McEwan said, coming out of her daze. "What did you say about Edward Derby?"

I didn't reply. Somehow, it seemed important that I place

that moment, the moment when someone recently inspected their hand.

Lisa said, "Ricky cracked Edward on the head and tied him up. But he escaped with John Davies. The police are on full alert right now."

Very dimly above the noise of the carnival, we could hear the sirens.

Mrs. McEwan looked at me sharply. "You knocked Edward Derby out?"

"He was kidnapping Mrs. Ghettley."

"This is terrible. I must get some fresh air, Ricky. And I must tell you something."

She walked slowly out the same door that Edward Derby had used to kidnap Mrs. Ghettley earlier. She sat on a bench on the outside of the school. Lisa and I followed. So far, our three-way conversation had been very private with the carnival in full gear around us.

"Sure," I said. "Would you like some water?"

"No," she said. "I mean yes. I mean I don't know." She ended with a moan. "Edward Derby? You knocked out Edward Derby?"

I nodded.

"It's John Davies, my former gardener, with the jewelry?"

I nodded again.

A part of my mind noted Mrs. Ghettley slowly wheeling her wheelchair along the sidewalk that led away from the school. Now that her attention had wandered from the carnival, I wondered sadly for her which world she was in now. Maybe like last Saturday when Lisa was pushing her back from the grocery store. A world with a cat named Madagascar. Then I gave my head a little shake. *A cat named Madagascar.*

"—not Edward Derby," Mrs. McEwan was saying.

That brought me back to her troubles. It must be terrible to discover your nephew is a fraud, especially at the same time all your valuable jewelry is stolen. Then it hit me. She shouldn't be disappointed in Edward Derby. He *wasn't* her nephew.

So I said, "Don't worry, Mrs. McEwan. He really isn't your nephew. I knew it all along, but I didn't want to say anything until I could prove—"

I stopped suddenly. From one edge of the playground, like a cat intent on a bird, Joel was beginning to sneak up on Mrs. Ghettley. There was a gap of fifty yards between them.

"Ricky, I knew it, too," Mrs. McEwan moaned. "I'm sorry I didn't tell you. It would have saved so much confusion. And maybe my jewelry."

I only half heard her. Joel was sneaking up on Mrs. Ghettley.

It sent alarm bells ringing in my mind.

And what else was nagging furiously in the back of my head?

Something about the wheelchair.

Mrs. Ghettley neared the far edge of the playground. Soon she would be to the corner of the street beyond.

"Edward Derby was an undercover private investigator brought in to save my jewelry," Mrs. McEwan was saying.

That totally registered. I gave my full attention to Mrs. McEwan and spoke very slowly. "Please say that again."

Mrs. McEwan took a deep breath. "Yes, a private investigator. I should have trusted you with it much earlier, but—"

Suddenly something else became much more clear and much more important.

"Lisa," I said tersely. "What color are your fingernails?"

Her brow furrowed. "What—"

I insisted almost wildly. "Quick. What color are your fingernails?"

She sulked slightly, then held her hand away from her and examined the tips of her fingers.

That was it!

I spun around and ran as hard as I could. If I didn't reach Mrs. Ghettley before Joel did, he might be dead within the next minute!

CHAPTER 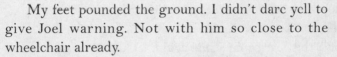 22

My feet pounded the ground. I didn't dare yell to give Joel warning. Not with him so close to the wheelchair already.

Look up, Joel! I wanted to shout, but I knew silence was the only way to save him. *Look up and see me running!*

Still a hundred yards for me to go.

I watched with horror as I pushed my legs harder. Joel nearly at the wheelchair and me so far away. His intentness and determination to carry out the last thing I had said to him.

"*Terrific,*" I had said. "*Now we have to find the funny man.*"

And there he was, Joel, my terrifying, frustrating, adoring, innocent brother about to reach out and tap the figure in the wheelchair the way he has tapped me a thousand times and scared me out of my shoes. Only this time the figure had a knife and deadly eyes.

I don't know when the tears started falling down my face. But the wind of my running whipped them back into my eyes. In the last seconds everything was a blur.

Go harder, legs! Oh, please go harder!

Joel was about to pounce forward. I screamed.

My scream carried with me as I dove across the last few yards into the wheelchair.

Shoulders into shoulders. The two of us tumbling onto the pavement in front of the sidewalk. My fingers into hair, eyes, nostrils, anything to keep that knife from Joel.

And suddenly I was yanked away.

I was delirious with anger and panic, and I sobbed and fought against the strong arms holding me back.

"Son! Are you out of your ever-loving mind!" Sergeant Brotsky roared at me. "Stop this instant or you'll be in jail forever instead of only the next ten years!"

I stopped and sobbed for more breath.

"Joel! Joel!"

"Son!" the roar came at me again. "There's no sign of the kid. And why you attacked a helpless old lady in a wheelchair I don't know, but it is enough to get you committed!"

In the heat and anger of emotion around me, I suddenly went limp.

"That's no old lady," I said. "Look under the shawls. It's John Davies. He's got a knife. He's got a knife and he would have k-k-killed my brother."

It was all I could get out. Then Davies did something that proved my sanity to them.

Still on the ground, he reached for his knife, but two patrolmen stepped on his wrist and pinned him there.

The Jewel of Madagascar rolled onto the pavement.

CHAPTER 23

"We thought you were crazy, bolting from us like that," Mrs. McEwan said as she wiped my face with a hanky. "In fact, I'm still not sure what happened."

The patrolmen had left with John Davies handcuffed in the backseat of their car. Sergeant Brotsky, Mrs. McEwan, and Lisa were standing with me in the shade of the oak trees.

The happy noise of the carnival leaked out from the open school door across the playground. It was hard for me to believe that no one at the carnival knew what had happened. Or that the carnival was still continuing. No matter. I would tell Mike and Ralphy later. *If* they forgave me for doubting their friendship.

"I thought I was crazy, too," I said. "But little pieces fell together, and when I saw Joel sneaking up on him, I knew he was in trouble."

I turned to Lisa. "Remember when I first told you that I wrecked some of Mrs. McEwan's jewels?"

"Sure," she said. "I was wheeling Mrs. Ghett— that is, John Davies, home from the grocery store."

"Her reaction was fine, for a senile lady. But *his* reaction, dropping the eggs, also made sense for a jewel thief, especially the way he stared at me when I talked about the Jewel of Madagascar. He tried covering up with a story about a cat named Madagascar."

"That's a pretty slim reason to tackle an old lady in a wheelchair," Sergeant Brotsky commented.

I smiled. "There's more, sir. Joel, who rescued us from Mrs. McEwan's basement, said he had watched a 'funny man.' I didn't think about it when he said it, but as I was watching him sneak up on John Davies in the wheelchair, I realized nothing would be funnier for him than seeing a man dressed in clothes like an old lady.

"Once it occurred to me that Mrs. Ghettley might be John Davies, the rest of it made total sense. Especially when Mrs. McEwan told us Edward Derby was an undercover private investigator. Who else could have hit me over the head when my back was turned to Mrs. Ghettley but Mrs. Ghettley herself? There was also the fact that Mr. Davies had been fired about a year and a half ago. I remembered that Mrs. Ghettley moved into town shortly after."

Lisa interrupted. "What was the stuff about fingernails?"

I laughed. "It's stupid, actually. Sergeant Brotsky, did I see gunpowder on your nails?"

He frowned slightly and examined them by cupping his fingers inward toward his palm.

"You just proved my point, sir. It's a little thing, but something that bugged the back of my mind. When women look at their fingers and fingernails, they tend to push their hands away from them and extend their palms outward while examining the backs of their hands. When men look at their fingers and fingernails, they do the opposite. They cup their fingers inward. In those moments as Joel sneaked up on John Davies, I remembered the way he had looked at his horrid red nail polish. Like a man. So I started running."

Sergeant Brotsky shook his head. "We should have guessed much earlier. Those heavy shawls all the time. A simple yet obvious disguise."

"We?" I asked.

"Yes," he replied. "We. I'll let Mrs. McEwan explain."

Mrs. McEwan spoke slowly. "When I realized my jewelry was stolen, I couldn't trust anyone. One by one, the real pieces of jewelry had been taken, then replaced with fake copies. It could only have been done by someone close to me. Which, unfortunately, included you, Ricky."

She sighed. "The worst part was that I was terribly, terribly underinsured. I had lost a fortune by the time I realized it had happened."

Lisa asked, "Wouldn't it make more sense for a thief to take all of them at once and run instead of going through all the work of getting fakes made?"

"Two reasons," Sergeant Brotsky said. "Obviously, a local person couldn't take the jewels and run. We'd know immediately who the thief was. A better way, then, would be to steal them without anyone knowing they had been stolen. The thief's problem was that glass replicas take a while to be made. The original jewel must be sent out of town and copied by an expert jeweler. So the jewels had to be taken out one by one and replaced in order to keep Mrs. McEwan from suspecting anything."

Sergeant Brotsky continued. "The other reason was resale. Antique jewelry is unique. It's too easy to trace a thief when he or she dumps it on the black market. But if the jewelry hasn't been reported as stolen, it's easy to sell."

"Yes," Mrs. McEwan said. "So when I reported my problem to Sergeant Brotsky, he said I should go on as if I didn't know they were stolen. Then the thief wouldn't be on guard as they tried finding him. Only it broke my heart to see Ricky so worried about having broken fake jewels."

I smacked my head. "I should have known. Glass fakes. *That's* why they smashed so easily. And why you had to tell me it was a fluke landing of the statue."

"Yes," Mrs. McEwan continued, "I couldn't let anyone

know that I knew about the fakes. Instead, Edward Derby told me it was a perfect opportunity to let more people know about the jewelry collection. Our plan was to make the collection as public as possible, especially so that everyone would know about the Jewel of Madagascar. We were using it as bait to bring the thief into the open."

I frowned a puzzled frown. "Some of this is making sense now. Especially the part about the secret passageways. More than once Edward Derby made it in or out of the house without me knowing how. He must have used those passageways."

"Ricky," Mrs. McEwan said, "I kept my jewelry safely hidden in an upper-floor passageway, all of them built of course by the crazy writer who lived there at the turn of the century. That was another reason I knew someone close to me was stealing the jewels. It had to be someone who had been in the house often enough to know about the passageways."

I said, "And I was one of those suspects, wasn't I? Even though you knew I was sick about breaking the jewels."

"Please take it as a compliment," Mrs. McEwan said. "A compliment that we thought you were smart enough to do it. Derby said if you were the thief, it would only be natural for you to fake that concern."

"Wonderful," I said.

"He said you were so innocent, it was a perfect cover," Mrs. McEwan protested. "But I wouldn't believe Derby until he told me about finding his suitcase disturbed and the way you ran into his room. He thought he'd almost caught you in the act. Especially with the secret passageway in that very same closet. After all, that's why I gave him that room. To have access to the passageway any time."

I explained why I had suspected Derby all along.

Sergeant Brotsky said, "When you came in with the glass to be fingerprinted, I didn't know who to believe. Derby was giving me reports labeling you as his main suspect, and *you* had good reason to doubt *him*. For a day, I thought maybe Derby was the jewel thief, *posing* as a private investigator! But then his fingerprints cleared him. So that left you as the suspect."

I remembered something. "But at the school, why did he steal the diamonds he was supposed to be guarding?"

"I'll answer that," a voice came from behind us.

Joel was leading Edward Derby along the sidewalk.

Sergeant Brotsky said, "Ed, are you sure you're fine to walk?"

"I've spent the last half hour on Mrs. McEwan's sofa. I should be fine. Especially with this little ghost here insisting I come over."

Joel blushed.

Derby continued, speaking to me. "That was some whack on the head, kid. Remind me not to make you angry again."

I blushed.

He said, "I made the diamonds disappear in school because the snake with the blue ribbon that popped from that kid's desk was a great distraction. I knew with the diamonds gone, I had a perfect excuse to ask Mr. Stanley questions about all of you. I was getting desperate to find the thief. You can imagine my shock when the diamonds were missing from my hiding place under the fire hose. In fact, where are they? Anybody know?"

"Um, Mr. Stanley has them. Joel found them first."

Derby grunted, wincing in pain. "It figures. Between the two of you, this has been my roughest assignment yet."

"Assignment! You were calling your boss the day I followed you to a phone booth?"

Derby grinned. "My wife. I wanted a little privacy."

I blushed again. "This morning you were kidnapping Mrs. Ghettley. At least, I thought you were. How did you have it figured out by then? And why were you taking him back to the house instead of to the police station?"

Derby made his shaky way to the curb and sat down. His face was still white. "The Jewel of Madagascar," he said. "I wanted it to be the Disappearing Jewel of Madagascar. And with the worm-eating carnival attracting most people in town, it finally did disappear."

The worm-eating carnival! Soon Mike Andrews would be in his booth, mouth open for those blobs of Jell-O. Thinking about it, I nearly felt bad about stopping by his house the night before. Yet there was no way I could leave until I heard the rest of this.

"You see," Derby explained, "the Jewel of Madagascar was also a fake. We even made up a legendary story about it to add realism. But it was a clever fake with a difference. Buried in the center was a transmitter. I wanted the jewel to disappear because I knew I could track down the thief as soon as he took it. And that, of course, would lead me to the rest of the jewels.

"So Mrs. McEwan and I left the house this morning, hoping the jewel would be stolen. And, as you probably have guessed by now, it was. And my directional finder tracked it down to Mrs. Ghettley wrapped in her shawls. I guess for John Davies, it was no problem to leave 'Mrs. Ghettley's' house, scoot up the secret passageways he had discovered while being a gardener, steal the Jewel of Madagascar, run back to Mrs. Ghettley's house, get in the wheelchair, and go to the carnival. No one would suspect her there. In fact, I could hardly believe it was her, even as my directional finder brought me right up to the wheelchair."

He stopped talking and smiled at Sergeant Brotsky. "Can you give me the finder back? It's an expensive piece of hardware."

Brotsky raised an eyebrow and tossed him the finder. Derby flicked a switch. A powerful beeping noise came to us. Brotsky grinned and reached into his pocket to show that the jewel was right beside us.

The sergeant said, "Right after Lisa's phone call, Derby staggered into the police station, telling me some kid who owned a crow had untied him. He was—"

"That was Joel," I interrupted. "He was untying everybody in sight."

"As I was saying, he was too hurt to chase down the jewel himself, so he gave me the finder. Only, at that point, since you were the one who whacked him on the head and tied him, Derby once again suspected that you were the thief, that maybe you had planted the Jewel of Madagascar on Mrs. Ghettley and were going to take it from her later. So I sent him back to Mrs. McEwan's house to rest and said I would try to find the both of you. When I saw you attacking Mrs. Ghettley, I assumed the worst about you, Ricky. That is, until I saw the knife."

One of the last things that had been bothering me finally made sense.

"That's how you managed to be exactly here as I tackled Davies," I said. "The finder brought you to the jewel, which he still had with him."

"Exactly," Sergeant Brotsky said with satisfaction. "Derby's a canny man. He didn't let Davies know that he had used a finder to catch up to him. After all, there still was the rest of the collection to be found."

"Right," Derby broke in with a quiet voice, "I was taking Davies back to the McEwan house, because he admitted he had hidden the rest of the jewelry in the basement. I didn't suspect anyone would rescue him—" he glared briefly at me —"in the manner they did."

"The jewelry was in the basement," Lisa said. "A brilliant place to store it until the day he was ready to leave town. We saw it where he had spilled it after tying us up."

Mrs. McEwan smiled and breathed heavily with relief, "All's well that ends well. I'm happy to have my collection back. Edward, you really earned your pay. Now, if you wouldn't mind telling me where they are, I'll find a safer place to store them."

Derby looked at Brotsky. Brotsky looked back.

"I thought you found them," Brotsky accused.

Derby's face grew even whiter. He stood quickly and held the back of his head. "You arrested the man," he accused. "I assumed you rescued the collection."

"It's an impossible job if the collection isn't on him," Brotsky shot back.

Mrs. McEwan quickly sat on the curb where Derby had been resting.

There was a full minute of terrible silence before she finally spoke.

"You gentlemen," she said with ice in her voice, "are not going to tell me the entire collection has disappeared somewhere and sometime between John Davies leaving my basement and this fine young man tackling him at the edge of the playground."

It was interesting seeing big, gruff Sergeant Brotsky pale at the tone of her voice.

"Ma'am—" he started apologetically.

"Hold it," I said. I knew where they were.

Mrs. Ghettley's wheelchair was still across the street, perched precariously over the opposite curb.

What had Lisa's words been? *Mrs. Ghettley was gone, Ricky. One handle of her wheelchair bent downward and some shawls left on the seat. Nothing else.*

Of course! The wheelchair handle was now straight!

All eyes were upon me as I strode across the street. For all the mistakes I had made so far, I could finally redeem myself.

I carefully felt the bottom of the wheelchair handle. Just as I hoped. A release button.

When it clicked, the handle fell downward. The hollow

tubing of the wheelchair was a perfect place to store diamonds and rubies.

I wheeled it back across the street and asked Mrs. McEwan to hold out her hands. Then with a grunt that reminded me of the throbbing at the back of my head, I hoisted the wheelchair into the air and flipped it over. I figured while I was being dramatic, I might as well have the jewelry cascade beautifully into Mrs. McEwan's hands.

Except nothing happened. The handle was empty.

It only took an instant for me to realize what was wrong with my theory.

"Joel," I said quietly with my eyes closed in frustration. "Where are the pretty stones?"

"He's gone," Edward Derby said with surprise. "Somehow he left without me noticing."

Down the street, I saw the last part of his shoe as he slipped into a hedge with, of course, the jewelry.

"Jooooeeeeellllllllll!" I shouted. "Joooooooooeeeeeellllll!"

It was no use. I started running.

EPILOGUE

It was a good thing for Mike that grown-ups have lousy aim. In fact, it was much better for him than he knew.

In front of him were all the people from the carnival. Most had tickets. The ones who didn't were there for the show. Ralphy regretted overlooking the fact that he could have charged for people to watch the worm eating.

Mike was sitting on top of the ladder, mouth wide open. He was wearing a bib and sunglasses to protect his eyes from Jell-O cubes. He wore a baseball cap backward to keep his hair clean.

By now the plastic on the wall behind him looked like someone had thrown buckets of red paint against it.

Lisa nodded to Ralphy for the fiftieth time.

He played a drum roll to make Mrs. Thompson's attempt seem dramatic. The whole thing, after all, was just a show. A fun show for everybody.

Mrs. Thompson grinned. Her first throw had hit the wall. Her second throw had bounced off Mike's left eye. The Jell-O was still hanging from his sunglasses.

The third Jell-O cube quivered between her

fingers. The worm inside it looked very real.

Drum roll again.

To add drama, Lisa began a radio commentary. *"Thompson checks the runner at first—slowly she arches back to set—she's in her windup—a frown of concentration—the delivery—the throw— bull's-eye! And the crowd goes nuts! Mike Andrews eats a mouthful of worm!"*

It was good. I have to admit it was very good. Seeing Mike Andrews fake a squint of agony and slowly choke down another worm. The worm throwers clapped and cheered encouragement.

It took half an hour to go through the big pot of Jell-O cubes. Mike ate nineteen worms. He got better at faking agony with each one.

Some people could hardly stand, they laughed so hard at his expressions. Me? My stomach felt queasy about the mistaken feelings I had had toward my friends during the week.

I still didn't know when would be a good time to confess.

Ralphy and Mrs. McEwan left to count the carnival proceeds. Since, of course, I was no longer in debt, we had decided to announce later that all the money was going to local charities. Mrs. McEwan had also said she'd pay me for my week's work, though not at one hundred dollars an hour, unfortunately.

Lisa and I began cleaning up. I wanted to talk to Mike about the worm-eating later—much later—not in the next few minutes. But he would not leave to wash his face.

"I'm fine," he said. Some of the red Jell-O was cracking on his cheeks. "I might as well help you guys while I'm still too mucked up to get any worse."

"Don't worry about it, Mike," I said. "You've done enough already. Honest."

"Are you kidding? I've never had a chance to fool so many people at the same time in my life. Licorice worms. Hah, hah. And they bought it hook, line, and sinker!"

"Yes. Um, why don't you go wash your face. Lisa and I will get this mess."

"Hey," he said. "How often do I volunteer to work? Take advantage of my good mood."

"It's okay, Mike. Really."

He wouldn't go. Mike began scooping Jell-O and worms off the plastic sheet beneath the ladder.

Lisa began stripping the red crepe paper off the ladder. I peeled the backup sheet off the wall. And worried about Mike.

The sheet fell off the wall and draped me, splashing Jell-O all over my clothes. That was the least of my problems. Mike had spotted what I didn't want him to spot.

"What's this?!" Mike yelled at me as I stood under the plastic. "I said, 'What's this?!'"

"Nothing," I said as I untangled myself from the plastic.

"Looks like a worm," Lisa said.

"It looks like a real worm," Mike hissed.

"I found a couple more of them," Lisa volunteered.

"It is a real worm!" Mike shouted. "How could this be a real worm!"

"I'm sorry, did you say something, Mike?" I asked.

Mike was an upset purple and no more words came out.

I smiled weakly at him. It generally takes Mike three or four minutes to cool down.

Mike began pawing the ground like a bull.

Then he backed me against the wall. Isn't it funny how people get stronger when they're mad?

"I, uh, wanted to talk to you about this, Mike. But it's difficult with your right hand around my throat."

"Lisa, find me some real worms," Mike said.

"Let's hear him out, Mike. It's got to be interesting." I instantly forgave Lisa for every time she has made me look stupid.

I explained quickly. "Now I know how wrong I was not to trust my friends. But yesterday I didn't. You and Ralphy had been acting strange all week. I overheard you mentioning the worms and I saw you buy them, so I dug up some real ones of my own, knowing you planned a major trick. Then I watched you guys until I had figured out what you might do with them. But I never figured on a carnival!"

He stared me straight in the eyes.

"Remember when you answered the front door last night but no one was there? It was me. But I was running to the back door, and I slipped into the kitchen and dumped all my real worms into the liquid Jell-O before you returned."

Suddenly I couldn't be serious about my apology anymore. I started giggling.

"I ate nineteen worms, and some of them tasted pretty strange," Mike said between clenched teeth. "Before I strangle you, let me remind you we *were* friends."

"We *are*," I said. "I nearly started crying when I realized what the Mike Andrews Worm-Eating Carnival meant. And you were having a great time fooling all those people, weren't you?"

Nothing about his baleful stare changed.

I pressed harder. "You always say pulling tricks is part of being friends. Remember? Tricks you both laugh about later. Like the time you told me Lisa's birthday was a costume party and I showed up in a banana suit. I was mad then, but it was funny later."

Mike slowly placed his other hand around my neck. I didn't struggle against it. He looked me dead in the eyes.

"And you"—he said slowly—"were the dumbest-looking banana I had ever seen appear at a formal birthday party."

Mike paused. "Unfortunately, this puts you one trick up on me. And you know how long it's going to take before I find this the slightest bit funny?"

I shook my head. Something hard to do with someone's hands around your neck.

"At least five more seconds," he muttered.

Then Mike sat down and howled with laughter.

Coming Soon!
Legend of the Gilded Saber

Ricky Kidd and his friends expect their vacation in Charleston, South Carolina, to be a boring history tour. But when Mike's uncle is accused of stealing a valuable Civil War relic, things start to heat up. As they try to prove his innocence, it is quickly apparent that the Accidental Detectives will get more than they bargained for!

Series for Middle Graders* From BHP

THE ACCIDENTAL DETECTIVES · by Sigmund Brouwer
Action-packed adventures lead Ricky Kidd and his friends into places they never dreamed of, drawing them closer with every step.

ADVENTURES DOWN UNDER · by Robert Elmer
When Patrick McWaid's father is unjustly sent to Australia as a prisoner in 1867, the rest of the family follows, uncovering action-packed mystery along the way.

ADVENTURES OF THE NORTHWOODS · by Lois Walfrid Johnson
Kate O'Connell and her stepbrother Anders encounter mystery and adventure in northwest Wisconsin near the turn of the century.

BLOODHOUNDS, INC. · by Bill Myers
Hilarious, hair-raising suspense follows brother-and-sister detectives Sean and Melissa Hunter in these madcap mysteries with a message.

GIRLS ONLY! · by Beverly Lewis
Four talented young athletes become fast friends as together they pursue their Olympic dreams.

MANDIE BOOKS · by Lois Gladys Leppard
With over five million sold, the turn-of-the-century adventures of Mandie and her many friends will keep readers eager for more.

PROMISE OF ZION · by Robert Elmer
Following WWII, thirteen-year-old Dov Zalinsky leaves for Palestine—the one place he may still find his parents—and meets the adventurous Emily Parkinson. Together they experience the dangers of life in the Holy Land.

THE RIVERBOAT ADVENTURES · by Lois Walfrid Johnson
Libby Norstad and her friend Caleb face the challenges and risks of working with the Underground Railroad during the mid–1800s.

TRAILBLAZER BOOKS · by Dave and Neta Jackson
Follow the exciting lives of real-life Christian heroes through the eyes of child characters as they share their faith with others around the world.

THE YOUNG UNDERGROUND · by Robert Elmer
Peter and Elise Andersen's plots to protect their friends and themselves from Nazi soldiers in World War II Denmark guarantee fast-paced action and suspenseful reads.

*(ages 8–13)

Expect Excitement and Adventure with the PROMISE OF ZION

Have you ever missed your family? Or wanted nothing more than to be home? If so, you'll identify with Dov and Emily in Robert Elmer's PROMISE OF ZION series. Set in Palestine before Israel became a country, these stories follow the adventures of two very different kids.

Dov is a thirteen-year-old Holocaust survivor who has been separated from his family and who dreams of being reunited with them. Emily, the thirteen-year-old daughter of a British official, is finding it hard to be away from England. As the world about them is thrown into chaos with the Jewish people trying to reestablish their home of Israel, the two become friends and try to help each other fulfill their ultimate dreams.

1. Promise Breaker   2. Peace Rebel   3. Refugee Treasure
4. Brother Enemy   5. Freedom Trap   6. True Betrayer

The Leader in Christian Fiction
BETHANY HOUSE